CHAOS IN HALIFAX

For Isabella,
Enjoy this true, and
devastating tale!
Cathy Beveridge

OTHER BOOKS IN CATHY BEVERIDGE'S
CANADIAN DISASTERS SERIES

Shadows of Disaster
(Ronsdale Press, 2003)

Stormstruck
(Ronsdale Press, 2006)

Tragic Links
(Ronsdale Press, 2009)

Chaos *in* Halifax

Cathy Beveridge

RONSDALE PRESS

RONSDALE PRESS
3350 West 21st Avenue
Vancouver, B.C., Canada V6S 1G7
www.ronsdalepress.com

Typesetting: Julie Cochrane, in Minion 12 pt on 16
Cover Art: Ljuba Levstek
Cover Design: Julie Cochrane
Author Photo: Andrew Platten
Paper: Ancient Forest Friendly Rolland "Enviro" — 100% post-consumer
    waste, totally chlorine-free and acid-free

Ronsdale Press wishes to thank the Canada Council for the Arts, the Government of Canada through the Book Publishing Industry Development Program (BPIDP), and the Province of British Columbia through the British Columbia Arts Council for their support of its publishing program.

Library and Archives Canada Cataloguing in Publication
Beveridge, Cathy
    Chaos in Halifax / Cathy Beveridge.

    ISBN 1-55380-019-2

    1. Halifax Explosion, Halifax, N.S., 1917 — Juvenile fiction.
2. World War, 1914–1918 — Nova Scotia — Halifax — Juvenile fiction.
I. Title.

PS8553.E897C43 2004   jC813'.6   C2004-904854-6

At Ronsdale Press we are committed to protecting the environment. To this end we are working with Markets Initiative (www.oldgrowthfree.com) and printers to phase out our use of paper produced from ancient forests. This book is one step towards that goal.

Printed in Canada by AGMV Marquis

For my parents, Donna and Pete,
who taught me the importance
of family

ACKNOWLEDGEMENTS

I would like to thank the staff of the Maritime Museum of the Atlantic, the Army Museum of the Citadel and the Public Archives of Nova Scotia. Special thanks to John Clarke of the Highlander Museum in Sydney, Nova Scotia.

Every attempt has been made to preserve the historical accuracy of the events surrounding the Halifax explosion. All the characters, however, are fictional.

A teachers' guide for *Chaos in Halifax* is available from Ronsdale Press.

Chapter One

Patches of sunshine dotted the departure lounge of the Calgary International Airport. Jolene and her brother Michael made their way among them, pausing to let a small electric cart pass. The driver, wearing a white cowboy hat and red vest, waved and smiled. Jolene watched the cart disappear behind a nearby smoothie bar and heard the whir of the engine cease. She veered right and two moving sidewalks transporting summer travellers came into view.

Michael sprinted towards them. "Race you to the washrooms," he cried, jumping aboard a black conveyor belt.

Jolene grinned. "Okay," she called, bypassing the moving sidewalks and crossing the corridor to the washrooms opposite.

"Hey! No fair!" Michael scrambled to run against the

motion of the sidewalk. He leaped free of the conveyor belt and joined Jolene outside the washroom doors. "Those people-movers are cool. We should have installed one between school and home."

"To save you walking a whole three blocks," said Jolene, grinning at her brother who trained seven times a week as a speed swimmer during the school year.

"Yeah." A smile stretched between Michael's dimples. He bent over the water fountain as Jolene pushed the door of the ladies room open. She held it ajar for an elderly woman clutching a small leather suitcase who was making her way out of the washroom.

"Thank you," murmured the woman. She shuffled past Jolene, the corner of the case jamming against the doorframe and twisting before thudding to the ground. "Oh dear!" The woman bent stiffly to retrieve the bag.

"I'll get that for you." Jolene reached for the leather case, but one of the handles had torn away. Grabbing the other handle, she tried to lift it, but the case was heavy. She felt the second handle strain. Quickly she set it down just outside the door. "One of the handles is broken."

Worry lines etched the woman's forehead. "It's not surprising, I guess," she said, surveying the damage. "That case is as old as I am." She looked up at Jolene and Michael, who had now joined them. "Why, you're twins!" A sudden smile replaced her look of distress.

Jolene joined Michael in a polite nod — their typical response to the predictable reaction of strangers.

"Can you carry it with just the one handle?" Michael asked his sister.

"The case is too heavy. The other one will rip."

A timid laugh escaped from the case's owner. "It's full of family photos, old cards and journals. The only things that really matter now." Eyes the colour of the ocean regarded them and Jolene felt a tinge of sympathy for the old woman.

"Do you have far to go?" asked Michael as his sister crouched down to examine the bag more closely.

Digging into her purse, the woman extracted her boarding pass. Holding it at arm's length, she strained to read it. "Gate 49."

Jolene scanned the corridor for the gate numbers. "At the very end."

The woman's polished black shoes shuffled awkwardly. "I should have checked it as luggage, but then I thought what if they lose it? All those things are irreplaceable."

Jolene glanced around the departure lounge. "It's too bad there isn't a trolley here." Her eyes lit up. "Where did that cart go?"

No sooner were the words out of her mouth than Michael was off and running in the direction of the smoothie bar. A motor whirred to life and the cart they had seen earlier drove into view. Michael was perched on the passenger seat beside the driver in the white Stetson.

"Your carriage, ma'am," he announced, leaping from his seat and indicating the cart with a dramatic gesture of his hand. The cart idled to a stop in front of them. The woman's

lips rounded in surprise, but she happily accepted the hand
Michael offered her and climbed into the vehicle. Jolene
slipped her hands beneath the corners of the case and
deposited it in the back compartment of the cart.

"How clever!" The woman's tiny hand still clasped
Michael's large one. "How charming and thoughtful." The
driver inched the cart forward. "Thank you," called the woman, releasing Michael's hand. She looked back over her
shoulder at Jolene and waved.

Jolene readjusted the straps of her backpack and watched
the moving cart with a mixture of satisfaction and irritation. The woman's praise and gratitude had been directed
primarily at her brother, despite the fact that the cart had
been her idea.

"That was easy!" Michael said, striding towards the mens
room.

Jolene pushed the adjacent door open, deep in thought.
Inside, she stopped to study her reflection in the mirror.
There was no mistaking that she and Michael were twins.
They had the same deep green eyes inherited from their
grandfather, the same features, the same dark wavy hair,
except hers was longer, reaching almost to her shoulders.
She had decided to grow it out this summer — and Gerard
had even commented on the change last time she had seen
him. The thought of Gerard made her cheeks flush and her
dimples appear. Tall, shy and soft-spoken, he had caught
Jolene's attention the moment he had arrived at their school
in February and been assigned to her table. He was differ-

ent from the other boys in their grade six class — older and more sophisticated somehow. And unlike all her other male classmates, he had gotten to know her before he'd become friends with her ever-popular twin brother.

Jolene pulled a tube of lip gloss from the small purse that hung over her shoulder. Everyone liked Michael and it was easy to understand why. His bubbly optimism was contagious and his happy-go-lucky nature made him easy to get along with, most of the time. She applied the raspberry lip gloss, making her lips shimmer in the fluorescent light. For the last six years they'd attended a small French immersion school. Most of their school friends were mutual friends. Jolene twisted her small crystal earrings and scrutinized her image. She smoothed her hoodie over the subtle curves of her hips. Next year would be different. In the fall, they would start junior high in a big school with students from all over north Calgary, with new teachers, new subjects and new friends. Friends who would know her as Jolene, before they knew her as one of the Fortini twins. She was looking forward to it.

Two middle-aged women entered the washroom and Jolene slipped back into the lounge, making her way to a nearby window. A big jet was rolling down the tarmac. Men with red vests directed the pilot, their ears covered, their hair whipping wildly about. Jolene watched as the nose of the plane inched forward until its door was aligned with the loading ramp.

"Jolene?"

She pivoted on her heel, her eyes scanning the lounge for the owner of that familiar voice, her heart thumping like a rabbit's foot. He was standing off to her left and she noticed immediately the look of happy surprise in his eyes. "Gerard!" She flitted towards him. He hurried to meet her and for a moment Jolene wondered if he was going to hug her, as he had the last time they had seen one another — a sudden, crushing hug.

"What are you doing here?" he asked.

"Flying to Halifax."

"But I thought you were in Kelowna."

"We were, until Dad decided that the museum needed a new exhibit. 'The more disasters, the better,'" Jolene said, quoting her father, who had recently opened a Museum of Disasters in Calgary.

"The Frank Slide exhibit was awesome," said Gerard, referring to the newest exhibit of Canada's deadliest landslide.

Jolene beamed. A few months ago she had been certain that the museum would be a disaster. That her father would regret having given up his engineering job to pursue his dream of creating a museum dedicated to the preservation of destruction. But that had all changed during their research trip to the Crowsnest Pass at the end of June. There, history had come alive and Jolene had discovered a way to bring it to life in her father's museum.

"Your grandfather is a great storyteller," added Gerard, as if he'd read her mind. "Will he be part of this new exhibit?"

"For sure," said Jolene quickly. That was the main reason

he was on this trip with them — to discover the story in history. "And the next one and the next one," she added fondly.

"I guess your dad's really into this now, eh?"

"Which is why I get to spend the next week researching the Halifax explosion."

"I've heard about that — some ship carrying a cargo of explosives collided with another one and the Halifax harbour sort of erupted." Gerard's fingers splayed outward from his fist.

"That's the one — Canada's most devastating disaster. It happened on December 6, 1917, during World War One." She fought the urge to trace the lines of Gerard's outstretched palm, tucking her hands inside the pouch of her hoodie instead. "Mom was flying to Halifax for a mathematics conference, so Dad decided we might as well all go."

"And I — " began Gerard.

"And you," she interrupted, "are travelling, probably on the same flight that we are, to Cape Breton to collect sea glass with your cousins who speak with a Scottish accent."

His smile uncurled like a lazy caterpillar in the sun. He moved closer so that their backpacks bumped. "And you," he said, gazing into her eyes, "have a very good memory."

He had told her his summer plans sitting on the grass around the outdoor pool, while they had licked frantically at their melting popsicles. "That's because," began Jolene, shifting her weight ever so slightly so that her shoulder pressed against Gerard's, "I always remember — "

"Hey Gerard, here's the change." Gerard's younger brother,

Scott, pressed a handful of coins into Gerard's hand. Jolene stepped back and Scott, his hair dyed a peroxide blonde, slipped between them. "Hey, I know you," he added, looking up at Jolene. "You're one of the Fortini twins." Jolene frowned as Scott plunked into a chair, a carton of chocolate milk in one hand and a bendable straw in the other. "I've got this great trick to show you." He forced the triangular top of the carton open. "I saw it on T.V."

"Saw what?" asked Michael's voice from behind Jolene's shoulder.

"Watch this!" Scott inserted the straw into the milk carton and bent its neck upwards. "First you suck the milk up into your nose and then you squirt it out through your tear ducts." He pulled his lower eyelid down to reveal a small opening at the base of his eyeball, surrounded by a network of bloody veins.

Jolene grimaced.

"I saw that guy on television," said Michael. "He made over two metres with one squirt."

"Out of his eyeball?" asked Gerard dubiously.

Jolene's stomach churned at the thought. But Scott had already inserted the straw into his nose, clamped his mouth tightly shut and plugged his empty nostril. Before anyone could intervene, he was sucking the dark, creamy liquid up into his nose. To Jolene's surprise, the liquid disappeared steadily until Scott suddenly coughed. His eyes bulged and his cheeks puffed. Chocolate milk spewed from his nose.

Gerard jumped backwards as milk spurted wildly from Scott's mouth, covering the younger boy's shirt, jeans and arms.

A loud laugh burst from Michael, drawing the attention of nearby travellers. Jolene looked away from the mess.

"Attention, ladies and gentlemen," said a voice over the loudspeaker system. "This is the first call for the boarding of flight 761 to Halifax. At this time, we would like to begin the preboarding of passengers with small children. All passengers must show photo identification at the gate."

"Great timing!" exclaimed Gerard as people in the lounge started to gather their things. Scott wiped his face with his shirtsleeve, leaving sticky brown streaks on his cheeks and chin. Michael erupted into another gale of laughter. Scott snorted and more chocolate milk oozed from his nose.

"Come on," Gerard ordered his brother. "Let's get you cleaned up." He gestured towards their backpacks. "Would you mind watching our stuff?"

"No problem," replied Jolene as the two brothers set off towards the washroom.

Beside her, Michael continued to chuckle. "That chocolate milk trick was the funniest thing I've seen in a long time."

"It was gross and immature."

"Gross, immature and hilarious."

Jolene's response was interrupted by a defiant meow. A tiny fuzzy white and black kitten had latched onto Michael's shoelace and was attacking it with great fervour. Its little body pounced back and forth with determination and energy. Michael bent down and scooped it up in one hand. The kitten looked up and meowed sassily.

"Oreo!" A girl's voice reached Jolene's ears from somewhere nearby, but she could not locate the speaker. "He's always escaping." Two copper-coloured braids emerged from underneath a row of chairs, followed by a pair of hazel eyes and a face covered with freckles. The little girl jumped to her feet and dusted off her denim skirt.

"What did you call him?" asked Jolene, totally absorbed by the presence of the tiny creature. Michael was stroking the kitten who was now purring.

"Oreo!" repeated the little girl. "See, his head and tail are black and he's white in the middle."

Michael held the little cat up to inspect it. "You're right!"

"What an adorable name," said Jolene. She stroked the sides of its face with two fingers and the kitten purred louder, stretching its neck upwards. "Isn't he cute, Michael?"

Michael shifted the kitten so that it was sitting in his hand. He scratched the soft silky fur of Oreo's belly. "Yeah," he admitted. He brought the little creature even with his face. "He's got those green cat eyes like a tiger." The kitten put one paw against Michael's lips, then stretched forward and licked his nose. "Hey, that feels like sandpaper," he protested.

"I better take him back to his kennel," said the girl with the freckles.

"Can I hold him first?" asked Jolene, plucking the kitten from her brother. She cuddled it against her, a dreamy smile on her face. The little girl held out her hands and, reluctantly, Jolene handed Oreo over.

Immediately, the kitten swatted at the girl's braids. "Come on, Oreo," she said, "we're going to take you on an airplane."

Jolene sighed. "Isn't he just the sweetest thing you've ever seen?"

"Yeah," agreed Michael. "He is pretty cute."

Jolene caught her breath. "Wouldn't you like one, Michael? A kitten like Oreo?" A couple of weeks ago, when their parents had finally agreed to a family pet for their upcoming thirteenth birthdays, Michael had immediately asked for a dog. But Jolene had given it a lot of thought and decided on a kitten. Mom and Dad had been firm. They could have only one pet, and only if they agreed on which one they wanted.

Michael's eyes followed the progression of the freckle-faced girl and her meowing package. He turned towards his sister. "I still think a dog would be cool, but I suppose having a cat would be okay."

Jolene leaped into the air. "Really? Really?" she asked. "You mean we can get a kitten?" She stood directly in front of her brother, her eyes levelled on his.

Michael tilted his head to one side. "Yeah," he said, "I guess we could get a cat."

Jolene threw back her head and spun around, "All right, all right! Oh, thank you, Michael, thank you, thank you." She grabbed his hands and squeezed his fingers.

"Stop that!" he protested, shaking his hands free and try-ing not to smile. "But I want a black cat — a witch's cat."

Jolene had had her heart set on a grey tabby. She hesitat-ed, but only for a moment. It didn't really matter what colour the kitten curled up on the foot of her bed was. "Fine," she agreed.

The voice on the loudspeaker interrupted her thoughts. "We will now board all passengers seated in rows twenty-one to thirty-one. Please proceed to the departure desk and have your identification ready."

As if on cue, Gerard and Scott emerged from the mens room and hustled towards them. "Sorry about that," said Gerard, gathering their backpacks. "Siblings can be so em-barrassing."

"I know," chimed Jolene's and Michael's voices simulta-neously. Jolene looked surprised, but Michael didn't notice.

"Do you remember that time, Jo, when I wore your un-derwear to school?" Michael dissolved into laughter while Jolene's cheeks turned a bright crimson shade.

"You wore your sister's underwear?" asked Scott in in-trigued disgust.

"Never mind," warned Jolene, starting in the direction of the departure gate. "We have to go."

"Yeah," answered Michael as if his sister had never spo-ken. "Her pink ones with tiny purple and white hearts and a lace waistband."

Jolene felt her face grow hot. It had happened years ago,

before Gerard and Scott had come to their school, and she'd almost forgotten about the whole incident.

"I had this micro-fleece hoodie and you know how they get all staticky in the dryer?" Scott nodded. "Well, Jo's underwear got stuck in the hood of my hoodie." Michael laughed loudly. "They fell out in the middle of Language Arts class and Ms Sorenson picked them up. She wanted to know whose they were and Jolene blushed so hard that everyone knew they were hers."

"Would all passengers seated in rows one to twenty-one please board the aircraft."

Jolene didn't look up. How could Michael be so insensitive as to tell that horrible, embarrassing story? "Those are our seats," she snapped, striding towards the gate. Michael hurried after her as did Gerard and his brother. Jolene's eyes searched the chairs where her parents and grandfather had installed themselves earlier. They were empty. Gerard and Scott headed towards the back of the line-up, but Jolene caught sight of Grandpa waving at her and Michael from near the departure desk. "Sorry," said Jolene, joining her grandfather and her parents. "Michael was . . ."

But Mom shook her head. "Later," she said. "Get your boarding passes out and have your photo identification ready."

Jolene dug her school identification card out of her purse and Michael pulled his, along with his boarding pass, from his wallet. Mom and Dad proceeded through the gate. "Oh no," gasped Jolene, rifling through her purse. "Maybe it's in my backpack." Michael shoved his wallet back into his jeans' pocket as she flung off her pack and unzipped it. Only her discman, her cds and a few books and magazines were visible inside. "I couldn't have lost it." That wasn't like her at all. She ran her fingers through her hair and racked her memory.

Grandpa and Michael had already passed through the gate. The lady behind the desk extended an expectant hand towards Jolene. Sweat beaded on her forehead. "I can't find my boarding pass," she stammered.

Suspicion clouded the woman's face. "I'm afraid that you won't be able to board without it," she said with serious eyes. "Are you travelling alone?"

"No," said Jolene, "with my family." She gestured towards the entrance to the boarding tunnel where her parents, her grandfather and Michael were assembled.

The woman took a few steps in their direction and addressed her mother, who returned with the attendant. "Try to remember the last time you had it," advised Mom, in her usual, logical manner. "Did you have it in the lounge when you and Michael were wandering about?"

"I can't remember." For the third time, Jolene stuck her hands into her jeans' pockets and came up empty. "I'm sure I would have put it in my purse, but it's not there." She blinked back tears. "What am I going to do?" The man behind her coughed impatiently.

"Calm down," said Mom. "It has to be here somewhere."

"It's in your pouch!" Michael's voice reached them from the entrance to the tunnel. Jolene's head snapped up. "In your pouch," called Michael again, pretending to slide his hand into an imaginary pouch across his stomach.

Jolene slipped her hand inside the pouch of her hoodie. A sharp paper edge nicked her finger and she pulled out her boarding pass, relief flooding over her. The attendant took it, along with her student card. She checked the two documents and then nodded, indicating that Jolene could join her family.

Clutching the pass in one hand, her cheeks burning for a second time that morning, Jolene scurried towards Michael. "Why didn't you tell me before?" she asked.

A look of bewilderment crossed Michael's face. "I didn't know that you were looking for it."

"And why else would I be searching through everything at the departure desk?" she demanded, brushing past him. "Didn't you notice that I was just a little worried?"

Michael shrugged. "Sure, but you're always a little worried these days," he said matter-of-factly before following her down the ramp to the airplane.

Chapter Two

Embarrassed, Jolene hardly looked up as a flight attendant leaned forward to read her boarding pass. "Seat
14F." Jolene glanced up at the numbers and letters above the
seats. F was closest to the window. At least that was good
news.

The line of people in front of her had ceased to move and
she waited impatiently in the aisle as a short lady in a camel-
coloured suit attempted to stow her luggage in the overhead bins. Behind her, Michael craned his neck to see what
the hold-up was. He dug a pack of bubble gum out of his
pocket. "Want some gum?"

Jolene shook her head. All she wanted was to find her
seat, sit down and forget the incidents in the lounge. What
must Gerard think of her now? Leaning forward, she tried
to look around the jam of people in the adjacent aisle to see

where he and Scott were, but she could see nothing. Jolene whirled about to look behind her, but the only thing visible was the sticky, pink bubble that Michael had just blown. Pop! The gum exploded in her face, leaving its wet, gooey remains in her hair.

"Oops!" Michael chewed on the remnants of the bubble on his lips.

"Michael!" Jolene's voice was a hushed roar. Her fingers clutched her hair, entwining themselves in the gluey mess. They came away flecked with bits of gum and saliva.

"We're moving," advised Michael, looking over her head.

Fuming, one side of her hair a sticky pink, Jolene glared at her brother. Then she turned and marched down the aisle to row fourteen. Grandpa was already seated in the aisle seat of the middle section in the same row. He looked up as she collapsed into her chair and flung down her backpack.

"What happened to Jo's hair?" asked Grandpa as Michael dropped into the aisle seat beside his sister.

"She made a U-turn into my gum."

"I did not!" seethed Jolene. She tugged at the gummy clump. "Michael popped his bubble in my hair." She held her hair straight out to let Grandpa see the damage.

A pair of jeans obstructed her view and she looked up. Gerard beamed down at her. One look at her face and his smile vanished. He looked distractedly away before continuing down the aisle. Jolene slumped down in her seat, wishing she could disappear.

"You okay?" asked Michael.

"Just stay away from me," she growled.

Michael made no response. Digging a magazine about BMX riding out of his backpack, he settled back into his chair.

Jolene reached into her pack and pulled out her hairbrush. She held a clump of hair out, trying to see the damage. Then slowly, methodically, she began the awful task facing her. When the last of the gum had finally been removed, Jolene put away her brush and shoved her backpack underneath the seat in front of her. She glanced at her brother who hadn't said a word throughout the whole procedure. He could have at least apologized.

All around them, Jolene heard the metallic click of seatbelts and the thud of overhead compartments closing. The murmur of voices intermingled with the background purr of the aircraft. Jolene buckled up and felt the plane lurch beneath her. They were moving. The nose of the aircraft swung around. She caught a glimpse of the plane's tail reflected in the polished windows of the terminal. A male attendant in a grey-green jacket with a starched white shirt was standing in the aisle beside the descending video monitors. A deep voice announced that the safety demonstration would now begin.

Jolene looked up at the video screen as the plane rolled steadily towards the runway. As each reminder appeared on the screen, she double-checked her seatbelt, ensured that her carry-on baggage was properly stowed, that her seat-back was upright and her tray table folded away. Then she turned her head to see the emergency exits over the wings, bumping Michael's magazine in the process.

"What are you doing?" he asked.

"Listening to the safety demonstration like we're supposed to be."

Michael closed his magazine. "If this thing drops out of the sky, we're toast." He re-opened the glossy pages to an article on trick riding, oblivious to his sister's annoyed look.

They taxied into position and the captain's voice, tinged with a French accent, ordered the flight attendants to assume their take-off positions. In the distance, Jolene could see silos gleaming in the sunlight. The plane was picking up speed and she felt the pilot nose the aircraft up and the wheels leave the tarmac. They seemed to skim the roofs of the warehouses.

Beside her, Michael shifted forward to look out the small sunlit porthole. "Lean back a little," he said as the plane's wheels retracted.

His request sounded too much like an order for Jolene's liking. She remained where she was, her eyes following the beetle-like traffic through the doll-like houses as the plane climbed.

"Come on," whined Michael, but Jolene ignored him.

They banked to the left and Jolene had a panoramic view of Calgary lit by the early morning light — the Calgary Tower dwarfed by the gleaming skyscrapers where her dad had once worked as an engineer, Talisman Centre with its white egg-shaped roof where Michael swam, and the slump-backed roof of the Saddledome where the Calgary Flames played. The river, winding like a long blue snake, grew smaller and smaller beneath them until they flew into cloud. She leaned back, allowing Michael a glimpse of white mist.

. "I get the window seat on the way back," he declared as they continued through the clouds.

Jolene made no reply. The seatbelt sign beeped and blinked off. A flight attendant announced that breakfast would be served shortly, followed by a beverage service. In the meantime, they would be distributing headphones.

Almost immediately, a blonde flight attendant with a permanent smile handed each of them a package. "Twins!" she noted, but neither Jolene nor Michael nodded politely.

Michael took his headphones and plugged them in. He switched the radio channels, finally choosing one and began to sing along to a popular tune. Jolene jabbed him in the ribs with her elbow. "Shh!" she whispered.

Michael pulled the headphones from his ears. "What?"

"Don't sing."

"Why not? I like the song."

"That doesn't mean you have to sing it on a plane!"

Michael screwed up his face. "It's no big deal. What's your problem anyway?"

Jolene yanked the travel magazine from the pocket in front of her. "We'll be teenagers soon, Michael. Hasn't it ever occurred to you that you should try to act like one?"

"And just what does that entail? Not losing your boarding pass?"

Colour crept into Jolene's cheeks. "No! It means showing some responsibility and good judgement. It means not telling stupid embarrassing stories or laughing at gross, disgusting tricks. It means acting your age."

"What!" challenged Michael. "In the last five minutes you've gone from following the safety demonstration like you've just turned thirty to behaving like some three-year-old and blocking my view." He paused, his voice low and even. "You're just mad because I told that underwear story in front of Gerard," he said, drawing out Gerard's name in a breathy, romantic way.

"No, I'm not!" she retorted. "And so what if I do like him? I'm almost thirteen."

"I know," Michael said slowly and deliberately, "and you've changed this summer." He turned his attention back to his magazine.

Jolene watched Michael out of the corner of her eye, her brother's words echoing inside her head. Maybe she had changed this summer, but what was wrong with that? She was almost a teenager; it was time to change. Jolene watched a cloud drift by and contemplated Michael's accusations. True, she hadn't exactly acted mature by obstructing his view on the take-off and she had probably over-reacted in the lounge. She felt a wave of remorse. She'd been angry and her emotions seemed to run wild these days. But it had all been so embarrassing — the underwear story, the board-

ing pass incident, the gum. Surely Michael could understand that. He would have reacted the same way if he'd been
in her situation.

She glanced sideways at her brother, knowing that he
would never have responded the way she had. They were, as
Grandpa always said, as different on the inside as they were
alike on the outside. She tended to be quieter, thoughtful
and creative. Michael, on the other hand, was outgoing,
upbeat and impulsive. Jolene sighed. And she had a tendency to care too much about what other people might
think of her. Still, Michael wasn't perfect either. He rarely
got mad, but when he did, he had a bad habit of holding
grudges. Jolene squirmed uncomfortably in her seat. He
was obviously holding one now. She knew that she owed
him an apology, but it wasn't easy with this angry silence
hanging between them. Maybe it was best to wait until he
cooled off.

Jolene opened the travel magazine and flipped to an article on Cape Breton. A winding road divided lush green hills
from sandy beaches. It was beautiful country — pristine
and powerful. She glanced at the caption. *Explore the magnificent highlands, hike unforgettable coastal trails, linger on
seacliffs that rise high above the sparkling surf.* Scottish names
that she could not pronounce dotted the map. In every corner of the page were pictures — men in kilts playing bag-
pipes, whales breaching, sailboats with their spinnakers billowing and the sun setting above a small fishing village. Cape

Breton, she knew, was the island where Gerard's Scottish ancestors had settled in the late 1700s and where his cousins still lived.

"How's it going?" Jolene turned at the sound of Mom's voice. She was leaning across the back of Michael's chair, but looking in Grandpa's direction.

Grandpa smiled at her and held up the book he'd been reading about the Halifax explosion. Ever since he had become the museum's resident storyteller, he had delved into history with even more than his usual enthusiasm.

"Have you learned everything there is to know about the explosion?" asked Mom.

"It's a fascinating story," he said, twisting his moustache. "Did you know that part of the anchor of the ship that exploded was found four kilometres away?"

Mom shook her head. "It must have been a tremendous force."

Grandpa held up a photo of a town in ruins. It reminded Jolene of scenes she'd seen on television of areas that had been bombed. "It was the closest World War I ever came to Canada, but not the closest Canada got to the war."

"No, that's for sure. We lost a lot of fine young Canadian men in that war," replied Mom. Jolene couldn't help noticing the solemn expressions on both their faces. Mom turned towards her and Michael. "And how are you two doing? Dad and I are a few rows back on the other side of the plane."

Michael hardly looked up from his magazine.

"There's a lady and a little girl with a kitten just in front of us." Mom smiled at Jolene. "You should come by and see."

"That's Oreo," Jolene informed her. "We met him in the airport." The memory of the little kitten attacking Michael's shoelaces leaped out at her. "And Mom, guess what?" She watched Michael who sat staring expressionlessly at a glossy page. "We've agreed on a pet for our birthdays." Michael's chin tilted upwards. "We're going to get a kitten. A black one," she added hurriedly.

Mom looked surprised. Grandpa had put down his book and was watching them. "Is that right, Michael? You've agreed to a kitten?" Mom asked.

Michael's eyes were fixed on the headrest in front of him. He tossed his head, stared meaningfully at Jolene and then turned to regard his mother. "I never said that," he declared evenly. "I've always wanted a dog."

Jolene felt anger explode inside her, flushing her cheeks a steamy red. "But you said," she protested. "You agreed."

"I did not," said Michael stubbornly. "I said we *could* get a cat. That doesn't mean we should get one."

Jolene clenched her jaw, a sense of betrayal overcoming her. "That's not fair!" Tears edged her words. "You said . . ."

"Never mind," advised Mom. "You've still got time to sort things out. Your birthdays aren't until the fall. But remember, we don't get anything until you agree," she reminded them before returning to her seat.

Jolene turned towards the window. They would never

agree. There would be no kitten. No fuzzy little fluff ball. "That's so unfair," she told Michael, her voice cracking with emotion.

Michael shoved his magazine into his backpack. "Yeah, well maybe you'd better figure out that you can't go around criticizing and blaming people and then expect them to do you any favours." He flipped open his seatbelt, stood up and stomped off towards the back of the plane.

Jolene let the travel magazine slide to the floor. Below her the clouds lay like huge cotton trampolines, glinting white in the sun.

"He does have a point." Grandpa had moved into the seat beside her. Jolene watched him tame his moustache.

"But he said we could get a kitten. Back in the lounge, he agreed and now . . ."

Grandpa pursed his lips. "You've been pretty tough on Michael today."

"I know," admitted Jolene. "And I should have apologized, but you know how he holds grudges."

"When you finally get him mad."

"He embarrassed me," she added, recalling Michael's story of wearing her underwear to school, "in front of my friends."

"Ah!" Grandpa said knowingly. "Well, that happens to everyone. It happened to me once, when I first met your grandmother."

Jolene looked up quickly. Grandpa's eyes held the look of

a story and that alone was enough to make her feel better. She relaxed into her chair as the sweet smell of blueberry pancakes reached her, making her stomach rumble.

"It was a fine spring day and I'd been out on horseback in the hills near town. The air was crisp, and the leaves still wore their lime-green coats. My horse was moseying down a deer trail when suddenly we emerged from the woods and there, on the hill opposite me, was a girl I'd never seen before. She had a blue dress on the colour of the sky. Her long hair was loose and as she twirled, it streamed out behind her like a fan of spun gold. She bent and picked a single flower — an orange prairie lily — inhaled its fragrance and then floated away as if her feet hardly touched the ground, as if she were walking on the sky."

A smile played on Jolene's lips.

"It didn't take long to find out who she was. Her family had just moved to town and in no time I knew her name was Emaline, that she was seventeen years old and that she lived in a cabin near the creek."

Grandpa's eyes were distant. "I wasn't the only young man in town who was interested in Emaline. The spring dance was coming up and I was determined to ask her to it. So I put on my best suit, slicked back my hair and returned to the lily patch where I picked a beautiful bouquet of lilies. Then, clutching them tightly, I marched down the hill towards Emaline's house. It was hot and I could feel my eyes watering, feel my palms sweaty and itchy. Even my throat felt tight, but I put it down to nerves. My heart was hammering and my breathing shallow by the time I reached the cabin. I marched up to the door and knocked. Emaline herself answered, looking mildly surprised. But her surprise turned to shock as I presented her with the lilies and then leaned heavily against a pillar of the porch, gasping for breath. 'I've come to invite you to the . . .' I managed to blurt out before I collapsed."

"Collapsed?" asked Jolene. "What happened?"

"When I came to, I was propped up in an armchair in the living room and Emaline and her mother were hovering around me, dabbing my arms and face with a mixture of baking soda and water. I was covered in red welts and my throat felt as if it were swollen shut. My eyes were watering and I was drenched in sweat."

"You're allergic to lilies?"

"Nope. I'm allergic to red ants and the flowers were crawling with them. So was I, for that matter. They'd crawled up inside my shirt and bit me all over." Grandpa laughed. "Your grandmother had to throw those lilies out, too."

"I bet you made quite a first impression."

"Did I ever. Funny thing was that she went to the dance with me even after all that. Then she was crazy enough to marry me."

Jolene smiled affectionately at her grandfather. "The sky girl," she said softly. "I always wondered why you called Grandma that." She leaned back, wondering if she would ever make that kind of a lasting impression on anyone.

The breakfast cart rattled towards them. Grandpa shifted into his own seat and Michael flopped down beside Jolene. "What's for breakfast?" he asked.

"Blueberry pancakes — Jo's favourite — or omelette," answered Grandpa, having overhead the flight attendant.

"Good," Michael said cattily, "I hope I get the last serving of pancakes."

Chapter Three

≈

Jolene managed to find Gerard after they'd landed, but she barely had time to say good-bye before he was whisked away by his boisterous Scottish relatives and she was led off to the rental car counter. "We're going directly to the Army Museum at the Citadel," Dad told them once he was on the highway. "That's where my cousin's son Tim works. I've made arrangements to meet him and pick up the key to our rental house."

Tim, whom none of them except Dad had ever met, had just finished renovating a house. It hadn't been rented yet, but it was furnished and he'd kindly offered the place to them for their short stay.

In the car, sandwiched between Grandpa and Michael, Jolene looked out at the scenery. There were more trees than she'd expected. In fact, from the plane, the land had seemed to be one wide blanket of green with shimmering patches of water. The highway they now travelled was a wide swath between conifers and deciduous trees. Signs on her right indicated the turnoffs to Halifax and they soon passed over a large toll bridge.

"That's Bedford Basin below us," said Dad. "The Halifax harbour is shaped like an hourglass and this is its top half." He indicated another bridge in the distance. "Over by that bridge is the middle, known as the Narrows, and beyond that on the way to the Atlantic Ocean is the bottom half of the hourglass."

They turned towards a cluster of highrises and hotels and drove alongside the harbour's edge. But Jolene couldn't see the shoreline. Huge smokestacks, massive ships and bustling dockyards blocked her view. A greasy smoky smell seeped through the open window. Mom turned her attention to the map and Dad navigated the car through the narrow, busy streets of downtown. They turned right and suddenly a large tower loomed before them.

"That's the clock tower," said Dad eagerly. "And the Citadel is just above it at the top of that grassy hill."

Jolene ducked her head to see the heavy stone walls atop the hill. Beside her, Michael twisted to see out the passenger window. "What is it?" he asked. "The Citadel, I mean."

"It's a National Historic Site now," said Mom, reading off the map.

"But it was first built as a British fort in 1749 to protect the city's inhabitants from the Micmac Indians," Dad told them.

"Too many scalpings, I bet," remarked Michael.

Dad squinted towards two flags flapping in the wind. "Over the years, four different forts were built as the city grew. The fort you see now was originally constructed in 1856 to protect against an overland attack in the event of a war with the United States."

"Funny thing was," added Grandpa, "the Citadel was never once attacked."

"Really?" Michael sounded surprised.

"Really," confirmed Grandpa. "But it did protect the city, at least the south side during the Halifax explosion of 1917. The hill and the structure of the fort deflected the force of the blast upwards, sparing a lot of homes and lives."

Dad stopped at a small booth just outside the Citadel. "We're here to see Tim Regent," he told the attendant. "I'm Doug Fortini."

The girl nodded. "He's expecting you," she said. "Park in the lot straight ahead and go up to the Army Museum. It's on the second floor of the Cavalier Building." She handed Dad a pass and he proceeded to the parking lot.

Jolene climbed out of the car and stretched. She followed Dad through a stone archway, past the information desk and out into the fort's huge courtyard. Arched and rectangular doorways dotted the high stone walls and people paraded atop the rampart past black cannons mounted on wheels.

"Oh look," said Mom, gesturing to their left. "There's a

fellow dressed like the soldiers must have been." Jolene caught sight of a young man in a bright red, high-necked woolen tunic with shiny brass buttons. A white sash hung diagonally across his chest, reaching to a green and blue tartan kilt. In his hands he held a long-barrelled rifle.

"Get a load of that hat!" remarked Michael. He was referring to a high feathery hat that seemed to grow out of the soldier's head before falling in a plume of feathers over his right ear.

"I believe it's called a feather bonnet," said Grandpa. He put one arm around each of their shoulders and pointed at Dad who was beckoning them from the second storey of the Cavalier Building beneath a sign that read *Army Museum*. They joined him inside the museum, which consisted of a series of small rectangular rooms.

"Why don't you have a look around while I find Tim," said Dad before disappearing into the adjacent room.

Jolene wandered through the displays — rifles, canteens, uniforms, helmets, pins — all labelled and dated. Mannequin soldiers stood in corners of the room and photographs told the story of the British garrison that had once resided there. She meandered into the next room and joined Grandpa who was peering into the glass display cases.

"This room is dedicated to the Nova Scotia regiments who fought in World War I," he told her as she joined him in front of a uniform belonging to Colonel Robert Borden. They moved onwards to a corner display where an ugly canvas mask, with alien-like eyeholes, hung. An accordion-style hose hanging down from the mask was attached to a canister covered in canvas. "That's a gas mask," said Grandpa behind her. "World War I was the first time gas was ever used as a weapon."

Beside the mask was a display of letters and photographs, showing masked soldiers looking like aliens. In one picture, a mask had been positioned over a horse's muzzle. "What was the gas?" asked Jolene, even though something in the pit of her stomach didn't want to know.

"Chlorine first and then others," said Grandpa. "Look, here's a report on the German gas shell." He skimmed the handwritten document, reading occasional phrases aloud. "A continuous rushing noise in the air, a white cloud that quickly disappears, the smell of mustard or garlic."

"What did it do to the soldiers?"

"It says here that they first experienced some irritation of the nose and throat followed by nausea and vomiting. Then the eyes became inflamed and they felt a searing sensation. Eventually, they were unable to keep their eyes open and unable to breathe." He sighed. "Slow suffocation in a burning blindness."

Jolene shuddered.

Grandpa pointed towards the gas mask. "The canisters contained charcoal," he explained. "It helped filter out the poisonous gases."

Mom and Michael joined them. "This is a pretty sobering display, isn't it?" said Mom. Jolene nodded.

"Why did Canada get involved in World War I?" asked Michael.

"Germany declared war on France and Britain was drawn into it as an ally of France. When the British entered the war, Canada, as a former British colony, was committed to follow her," explained Mom.

"How many Canadian soldiers died?" asked Michael.

"We lost sixty thousand," replied Grandpa.

The number was staggering. Jolene tried to imagine a graveyard with sixty thousand graves.

Moments later, Dad arrived with a thin man in his early thirties, sporting a brown, bushy moustache. "I'd like you to meet Tim," he said by way of introduction. "Tim, this is my wife, Kate, my father, Victor, and my children, Michael and Jolene."

One by one they shook hands while Tim twitched his moustache at each of them. Jolene thought he resembled a squirrel. "I think we've got the accommodation all sorted out," boomed Tim. The force of his voice made Jolene jump. "The site doesn't close for another twenty minutes. The modern day Citadel recreates the time period of the 78th Highlanders. If you'd like, you can have a quick look around while I collect the keys for Doug." He smiled then tugged on his moustache, pulling the corners of his mouth back down to a thin line.

"Good idea!" said Dad. "You may as well see the Citadel

while we're here." He hurried after Tim who had already scampered down the staircase.

"Come on," said Mom leading the way across the courtyard. She ducked into a narrow room furnished with long wooden tables and benches. A coal stove stood near a solitary desk at the front of the room and chalk slates decorated the tables. "This must be the schoolroom."

Jolene regarded the room curiously. A large frame with rows of beads on wires stood on a nearby table. She slid the beads towards one end of the wire. Beside her, Michael picked up an empty slate and a piece of chalk and wrote *I was here.* "Come on," he called looking around. "I want to go up on the rampart." He darted out the door.

"I'd better go with him," said Mom. "We'll meet you two back in the courtyard at closing time." She dashed off in the direction Michael had taken.

Grandpa moved deliberately around the schoolroom, stopping to peer at an early map of the world and then joining Jolene in front of the frame with the beads on wires. "That's an abacus. It's used for doing mathematical calculations."

Jolene slid three more beads along the wire. "I think I'll stick to my calculator." She picked up the slate Michael had written on, a frown crinkling her forehead. With a brush, she hastily erased his words and set it back down beside another slate bearing the message *Family ties are unbreakable.*

"It's true, don't you think?" asked Grandpa pointing to the slate.

Jolene shrugged. "I don't know, Gramps. Sometimes family ties are unbearable."

Grandpa threw back his head and laughed. They stepped out of the schoolroom into the sunny courtyard. "I remember the first day you and Michael started kindergarten. I'd taken you to school because your folks were working. When we arrived, we discovered that there were two classes and the principal had decided to split you up." He smiled, remembering. "The two of you stood in the corridor, holding hands, with both your teachers trying to coax you into their respective classrooms. And then you announced, in no uncertain terms, that you would not be separated." Grandpa's chuckle was deep and throaty. "You just stood there clutching hands and looking so determined that eventually they put you both in the same class. You and Michael have been in the same class ever since."

Jolene kicked at a pebble in the courtyard. "We probably won't be next year."

"No," agreed Grandpa. "Does that worry you?"

Jolene shook her head. "Actually, I'm looking forward to it." A look of surprise crossed Grandpa's face, but before he could speak, a lone drummer dressed in the uniform of the 78th Highlanders marched into the courtyard and began a rapid drum roll.

A group of curious onlookers encircled him, but Jolene could not spot Michael or their mother.

"Let's go up on the rampart," suggested Grandpa. "Maybe we'll be able to see them from there."

Jolene and Grandpa surveyed the courtyard from up above but couldn't find the others. A platform in one corner offered them a spectacular view of downtown Halifax and the harbour. A sailboat, its white sail glistening, passed an outgoing freighter. Jolene followed the sailboat's progress as it glided past a small island, ducked under the bridge she'd seen earlier and disappeared through the Narrows. "The farthest point on this shore visible from here is called Point Pleasant Park," a guide explained to his tour group. "The large island just off the point is McNab's Island."

The tour group followed their guide towards another corner of the rampart and Jolene meandered along behind Grandpa. "It's pretty, isn't it?" she said, looking out at the glimmering water, but Grandpa did not respond. He was standing riveted in front of a small opening in the stone wall. "Gramps?" Something in his expression made Jolene's heart beat faster. She had seen that look in his eyes before — in a mine tunnel in the Crowsnest Pass. "Gramps," she repeated in an excited whisper.

He turned blank eyes towards her, blinked and swayed. She put out a hand to steady him. "What is it?" she asked, peering past him.

Grandpa pointed through the opening in the wall. "Have a look," he said softly. "Out there." A warm breeze rustled Jolene's hair.

The grassy slopes surrounding the Citadel were covered

in people, their clothes torn and filthy. A man, his face covered in a slimy black sludge, carried a young girl in his arms. Blood matted the girl's blonde hair and Jolene could see a deep gash on her head. "We need a doctor," he cried at the heavy doors of the Citadel.

A woman limped towards him, one eye bandaged. "Open up!" she called.

"What's happening?" asked Jolene.

"After the Halifax explosion, many of the wounded came to the Citadel seeking aid," explained Grandpa.

A group of men joined the others at the doors of the fort. "We need food and shelter and medical aid," they cried. People flocked to the gate and pounded on the wood. Slowly, the heavy gate opened and the wounded were carried through the beehive-like entrance. A shivering child, his lips blue, moaned as a man lifted him from where he lay on the grass. An elderly woman, her face sparkling from the slivers of glass embedded in her cheeks, was ushered through.

"What's going on?" Michael's voice crashed through Jolene's thoughts. She spun about and Grandpa jumped. Michael stood behind Jolene's shoulder, peering at the opening. "Where did all those people come from and why are they dressed so funny?"

Grandpa watched his grandson's face carefully. Jolene looked back through the opening. A group of tourists wearing bright yellow vests were now marching up the steps past the clock tower. Is that what Michael had seen? Michael looked momentarily confused. From inside the courtyard came a loud barking order followed by the marching of boots.

Jolene shifted nervously. "Where are Mom and Dad and that loud squirrelly guy?"

"Waiting for us below," replied Michael, laughing. He raced down the staircase.

Jolene hung back, sauntering slowly along beside Grandpa. "Were we looking into 1917?" she queried.

"Hours after the explosion."

Tim was talking as they joined the group. "Many injured and homeless people flocked to the Citadel following the explosion," he told them. "The wounded were treated by the regimental surgeon and others were given temporary shelter from the snowstorm that followed."

"That must have been what was happening outside," said Michael. "That's why all those people were dressed up like they were hurt. For some kind of re-enactment."

Tim looked perplexed. His moustache twitched.

"Well," said Grandpa quickly, "it looks like closing time." All but a few straggling tourists had sauntered out the main gates. "It was nice to meet you, Tim."

"My pleasure."

Dad shook Tim's hand. "I'll be in touch," he said before Tim scampered away.

Jolene trailed behind the others and Grandpa fell into

step beside her. "Michael could see those injured people."

He was, she knew, simply stating the facts. Michael had been able to see into the past and witness the drama on the Citadel slopes as it must have unfolded in 1917. "I know."

"So, not everyone can. You know that your dad can't, for example."

"I know," repeated Jolene.

"That probably means," said Grandpa, "that like us, Michael can — "

"I know!" said Jolene, not wanting to hear what she already knew. With a long sigh, she kicked at a pebble and sent it skimming across the courtyard.

Chapter Four

Sunshine streaming through the vertical blinds streaked Jolene's blankets and caressed her face. She stirred then opened her eyes as a piercing whistle invaded her slumber. "What is that? A ship?" she asked, propping herself up on the pullout couch in the living room and brushing the tangled hair out of her eyes.

Grandpa adjusted the suspenders he always wore and chuckled. "Just a tea kettle, I'm afraid. I didn't know it sang," he added apologetically. He poured steaming water into a mint green mug.

"That's okay, Gramps." Jolene squinted towards the window as Grandpa made his way across the room and opened the blinds. From her bed, she could see the glistening waters of the harbour. "It's a beautiful morning."

"It is," agreed Grandpa. "And it's even nicer outside."

Jolene laughed then yawned. Smiling, she watched her grey-haired grandfather sip his tea. When he had first come to live with them a few months ago, it had been because her parents had thought he was losing his mind — telling stories about places he couldn't possibly have visited and sights he couldn't possibly have seen. Except he had. Sights like they'd seen at the Citadel yesterday.

Sights like she'd seen in the Crowsnest Pass when Grandpa had first shown her a window into history. Her father had been there with them, but unable to see the coal miners working a century ago. According to Grandpa, who had initially discovered the family secret in Jolene's great-great-grandfather's journal, it all had to do with their ability to feel and understand the energy of history. It was that energy that had created the time crease that had drawn them back into coal mining history and made them temporarily a part of pioneer life before Alberta had become a province. It was that energy that had sent Jolene on the most exciting and risky adventure of her life.

Yesterday at the Citadel, Michael had been able to see through the window into 1917. That meant that he'd likely be able to slip through time creases with them. Her brother hadn't been with them in the Crowsnest Pass. He'd been in Vancouver at a swim camp, but he was here now. And yet, for some reason she didn't fully understand, Jolene didn't want to share their secret with him — at least not yet.

She sat up and dangled her legs over the side of the pullout, watching Grandpa twirl his moustache between sips of tea. His moustache and his stories had delighted her and Michael since she could remember. Reaching into her suitcase, she extracted a pair of comfy shorts and a white tank top. "I think I'll have a shower," she said. "Then maybe we can make plans for today."

"Plans?" asked Grandpa.

"Plans!" repeated Jolene. She glanced at the closed door of the bedroom Michael and Grandpa shared. "How far is the Citadel from here?"

"A long walk."

Jolene shrugged happily. "It's a nice day for a walk." She rummaged through her suitcase for her shampoo, wondering what Dad had scheduled for today.

"Morning Gramps!" Michael stood in his bedroom doorway, one side of his hair flattened against his head, the other sticking straight up. "Nice hair, Jo!" he added, gesturing towards her tangle of curls and waves.

"Thanks," said Jolene, grinning. "It looks just like yours."

By the time Jolene had showered, Dad had arrived home and put away the groceries he'd picked up after dropping Mom at the university. Now he bustled about the kitchen, collecting and washing up dishes. "I've got a surprise for you all," he said excitedly. "I've reserved spots on a harbour cruise this morning. The boat will take us all around the Halifax harbour right from Bedford Basin to the site of the explosion, over to the city of Dartmouth on the other side, and out past McNab's Island to the Atlantic." He beamed at them.

"What kind of a boat?" Michael's spoon stopped in mid-air.

"It's a sailboat, although I think it also has a motor," said Dad.

Michael's eyes lit up. "All right!"

Ever since their uncle in Vancouver had taught them to sail two summers ago, Michael had been crazy about boats.

"I think I'll have to pass," said Grandpa, draining his mug. "I'm afraid my sea legs have abandoned me in my old age. Not that they were ever very good."

"I forgot about that." Dad smiled at Jolene and Michael. "At least you two don't get seasick."

Jolene dried her hair with a towel. She liked boats and the harbour tour sounded exciting, but if she stayed with Grandpa, maybe they could go back to the Citadel. "I think I'd rather stay here with Gramps," she said, avoiding looking at Dad who, she knew, would be disappointed.

"Really?" he asked. "I thought you'd be excited to go."

"Yeah," agreed Michael, "especially since you didn't get to go to sailing in Vancouver this year." Michael had spent a week with their cousins on the west coast after his swim camp. Normally, the whole family vacationed out there and Jolene loved the sea and surf, but today she wanted something else — independence and a chance to make her own decisions.

"Don't stay on my account," insisted Grandpa. "I don't get bored easily."

How could anyone be bored in another time period? Her decision was made. "I didn't sleep very well," she told Dad to soften the blow. "I'd prefer to stick around here with Gramps."

A look of concern flashed across Dad's face. "Okay," he said. "Try and get some rest." He picked up the car keys. "We'll be back around 2:30."

After Dad and Michael had left, Jolene shoved her lumpy bed back inside the couch and replaced the cushions. "Can we go exploring?" she asked Grandpa, her mind racing ahead of her speech.

"I thought you weren't feeling well," he said suspiciously.

"I didn't say that," she replied honestly. She bounced across the room towards him. "Can we go back to the Citadel, back to 1917? Please Gramps?"

Grandpa shook his head. "It's a long way, Jo, and I don't have a map." Jolene looked disappointed. "But there's lots to see and do around here," he continued. "Come on, let's take a walk."

Half a block from their rental house on Kaye Street, Jolene paused beside the steps of a rust-coloured brick church decorated with a large rectangular plaque. It was dedicated to the memory of all those who had perished in the Halifax explosion on December 6, 1917. She looked around the neighbourhood. "Was this area damaged in the explosion?"

"This area," said Grandpa, "was devastated by the explosion." He squinted into the sunlight towards the harbour. "When the ships collided, the munitions ship drifted in towards Pier 6 not far from Richmond Hill, which is where we are now."

Jolene peered down their tree-lined street as if seeing it for the first time. It descended steeply towards the harbour past modest homes with porches. Vivid flower gardens surrounded the houses. Children's voices called to each other in the yards, and teenagers on bicycles and skateboards darted across intersections. It was hard to imagine that on a December morning in 1917, there had been nothing here but ruins.

They turned and ambled along Albert Street. Jolene looked out towards the harbour. "We're quite a distance from the water," she observed. "That must have been a huge explosion."

"The *Mont Blanc*, the munitions ship," explained Grandpa, "was carrying 2400 tons of explosives in its hold. It also had barrels of benzol, a highly explosive gasoline, on deck. When the *Imo*, a Belgian relief ship, collided with it, a spark from the metal scraping on metal ignited the barrels on board the *Mont Blanc*. Once the temperature on board the ship became hot enough, the entire cargo hold filled with explosives erupted. It was the biggest manmade explosion until the bombing of Hiroshima during the Second World War."

Jolene turned wide, incredulous eyes towards Grandpa. He continued. "The heat generated by the blast was so great that the people closest to the ship were vaporized." Grandpa began the steady climb up Richmond Hill. "The shock of the blast was felt up to four hundred kilometres away."

Jolene let out a low whistle. "No wonder it was Canada's greatest disaster."

A grassy plateau awaited them at the top of the hill, with a sign welcoming them to Fort Needham Park. An enormous granite tower stood amidst soccer fields and baseball diamonds. Jolene was not surprised to learn that the monument was dedicated to those killed in the Halifax explosion. She scanned the long list of alphabetically arranged names, lingering on whole families consisting of dozens of people. "How many people were killed?"

"Almost two thousand, and another nine thousand injured." Grandpa paused. "Never mind those who were homeless or orphaned."

The day was hot and suddenly the sun seemed particularly piercing. Jolene followed Grandpa across the park and back down the hill towards their house, which was only a few blocks from the harbour. "If this area was devastated by the explosion," she asked cautiously, studying both sides of the street, "how come there aren't any time creases?"

Grandpa stopped in front of the rust-coloured church they had passed earlier. "There are."

Jolene spun around, her eyes darting from shadow to

shadow, looking for the dense hot shadow that marked a time crease. They all looked the same, like ordinary shadows. "Where are they? Can we go back? Why didn't—"

"Whoa!" said Grandpa. He raised one hand to silence her. "Why are you so anxious to go back anyway?"

"Because it's new, I mean old, and exciting and because," she admitted, "nobody knows me there." In the Crowsnest Pass, she had disguised herself as a boy and learned to become a risk-taker, daring to do things she had never had the courage to do before. "I can be whoever I want to be."

"And just who would that be?" queried Grandpa.

"Me, my real self — whoever that might be." She paused in thought. "Michael says I've changed this summer."

Grandpa played with his moustache. "Well, you've let your hair grow and pierced your ears and sometimes your emotions run like a roller coaster. So, I guess I'd have to agree."

"Do you think it's a bad thing?"

Grandpa chuckled. "No, it's a natural thing. You're at that age when you need to discover how to be your own person. Everyone goes through it."

"Did you?"

"Sure, and it can be confusing." He brushed an unruly wave of hair out of her eyes. "Your folks have given you a good set of values to build on, but now's the time when you start to question things for yourself. It's part of constructing your own sense of who you are."

Jolene tugged at her hair. "It's weird, but in the past, when I meet people, it's almost like I get to know myself at the same time they get to know me."

"Our experiences and circumstances make us constantly re-evaluate things. It takes a long time to figure out who you are and what you stand for in life."

"Then I'd better get an early start," joked Jolene. "Now, can we go?"

Grandpa's expression grew serious. "The Halifax explosion was no laughing matter, Jo. Our rental place is right in the heart of the devastation." His eyes narrowed. "After nearly being buried by the Frank Slide, I'm not so keen to take those kinds of risks here."

"So you don't want to go back in time?"

Grandpa didn't answer right away. "I didn't say that," he said, watching Jolene's face light up, "but I don't want you getting hurt either." He tugged at his suspenders. "You can go back, but only with me when I know it's safe. Is that clear?"

Jolene jumped up and down on the sidewalk. "Crystal clear," she agreed. "I promise."

A reluctant smile emerged from beneath Grandpa's moustache. He checked his watch. "Your dad and brother won't be back for another two hours," he told her. "Follow me."

Jolene bounded up the stairs of the church beside Grandpa. "You mean there's a time crease right here?"

Grandpa led the way across the lush lawn and around the

side of the building towards a dark shadow. "Do you remember how to time travel?"

"I think so." The shade grew denser. It felt warm and tangible and alive. Jolene clutched Grandpa's hand and closed her eyes. "I'm thinking of myself as stationary in time at this location," she said, remembering the first time she had time-travelled. "I'm letting the energy of the time crease pull me through the ribbon of time." A warm breeze hit Jolene as the darkness grew deeper, darker and denser. She began to feel her body stretch as if it were being pulled apart like an elastic band. She strained to breathe. And then suddenly, a hot blast of air knocked her off balance. She fell forward into the light.

The summer green lawn was gone, replaced by frozen dirt. A cool gust of wind made goose bumps appear on her bare arms.

Beside her, Grandpa was doubled over, inhaling deeply. He stood upright and smoothed his hair back. "Well done," he praised her.

Jolene's smile stretched between her dimples. "Hey," she said, "the church is still here."

"I suspect this is the original one."

Jolene's teeth chattered and Grandpa turned his attention to her clothes. "We had better do something about your modern summer attire."

"Could we borrow some things from a clothesline like we did last time?" she asked.

"Maybe," said Grandpa. He twirled his moustache as he often did when he was thinking hard. "You stay here. I'll be right back."

Jolene watched Grandpa duck around the side of the church. Moments later she heard a woman's voice. "Why, I bet you're from the orphanage, aren't you?" The voice didn't stop talking long enough for Grandpa to answer. "The Reverend's been expecting you and I only just made it in the nick of time with these garments. We thought you were coming next week, but I expect you have to come when you can." Jolene heard the church door being propped open and crept towards the corner of the building to hear.

"Everything's right here in this trunk in the lobby. Makes it right convenient for parishioners to drop things off. The Reverend's always thinking of things like that." Something creaked and Jolene imagined the lid of the trunk being opened. "We've collected quite a few things, not new, mind you, but still with lots of wear left. I'm sure those poor children will appreciate them with winter fast approaching, too."

"I'm sure they will," replied Grandpa's voice.

The woman, her hair protruding from under her hat, emerged from the church lobby and surveyed the street. Jolene shrunk back against the wall. The woman had a large, sturdy build and was dressed in a heavy brown skirt that hung below the fur trim of her long coat. "Don't tell me that they sent you without a wagon?" She spun on her heel and shook her head. "I don't expect you'll be able to manage that trunk on your own." Jolene heard the tapping of her shoe on the concrete.

"No, I don't suppose I will," replied Grandpa honestly. "Perhaps I ought to take the things we're most in need of today and leave the rest until a wagon can be found."

"A fine idea!" exclaimed the woman. "Now if you'll excuse me, I must find the good Reverend." Jolene heard the clicking of the woman's shoes receding. "I expect you'll find a bit of everything in there — almost anything for any age," the woman added.

Minutes later, Grandpa appeared around the side of the church with an armload of clothes and a wide grin. "I ran into Lady Luck," he said, handing her a long pleated skirt, a worn petticoat, a white blouse and a navy woolen coat with gold buttons. "You can probably slip those things over your shorts and top."

Jolene did so, pulling on the petticoat and skirt first, followed by the blouse. Methodically, she did up the row of tiny buttons on the front and flattened the blouse's large circular collar, which covered her shoulders. Grandpa held the coat out for her and she slipped her arms into it. Two of the gold buttons were missing but she was glad of its warmth. Her coat reached to her knees and her skirt to mid-calf. She stood looking down at her purple flip-flops.

"Uh, oh, those will not do." Grandpa disappeared again and returned with a pair of black lace-up boots. "They're a little worn, but I think they'll fit."

Jolene shook off her flip-flops and slid her bare feet into the boots. There was a ridge in one of the soles and they were slightly on the large side, but they'd be a lot less conspicuous than her flip-flops. Grandpa had already donned a woolen jacket and cap and was looking as if he were going to work at the museum. "Well?" she asked spinning around in the bulky skirt.

"Just one more thing." He positioned a flat, grey, knit hat with a large pompom on her head. Jolene raised her eyes skeptically. "They're all the fashion," Grandpa assured her.

Using a church window as a mirror, Jolene adjusted the wide knit hatband and tilted the hat to one side. She turned back to face Grandpa.

"Perfect!" he announced. "Shall we go?"

Jolene tucked her flip-flops behind a bush and stepped into the sunshine with a broad smile. "Follow me."

Chapter Five

Jolene chose the same route they had followed in the present and soon the field of Fort Needham stretched ahead of them, its plateau falling to steep hills on one side. The playing fields had vanished. So too had the monument dedicated to the victims of the Halifax explosion.

Jolene surveyed the wide-open space, feeling a sudden longing to run. A group of children were playing on the opposite side. She could hear their voices rise then disappear, stolen by the gusting wind. Grandpa pointed towards a rough wooden bench near a stand of trees. Two men in woolen uniforms occupied one end of the bench. The older one looked up as Grandpa and Jolene approached.

"Good day," said Grandpa, tipping his cap.

"Good morning," replied the older man in a gravelly

voice. Deep creases lined his forehead as if someone had freshly sculpted them. He folded the newspaper in his hands and slid over towards the young soldier beside him.

"Are you just back from active duty?" Grandpa asked, sitting down. Jolene perched on the end of the bench.

The hazel eyes of the old soldier hardened then softened. "I came back this spring," he said plainly, holding up his right hand, which was missing three fingers. Jolene stared in horror at the shiny, smooth, red stump of his hand. "Andrew returned after Ypres." The young soldier beside him did not turn at the mention of his name.

"The whoosh of a kite?" The abrupt question caught Jolene off guard. It was Andrew, the young soldier, who had spoken. He had lifted his chin and was pointing towards the sky.

"A kite riding the wind like an eagle," confirmed the older soldier. Two boys had just run over the top of the knoll, holding a kite, its tailing whipping about in the wind. Andrew smiled happily. "Andrew used to come here as a boy," the older man told them. He shifted and extended his disfigured hand. "Major Robert Thurman."

Grandpa shook the outstretched hand, seeming not to notice the missing fingers. "Victor Basso," he said, adopting the same name he had used in the Crowsnest Pass. "And this is my granddaughter, Jolene."

Major Thurman nodded in Jolene's direction. She smiled nervously, relieved when he did not offer her his stumpy hand. "Andrew was one of my boys at Ypres," he said proudly, patting the young soldier's shoulder. A blank expression haunted Andrew's face. Major Thurman extracted a pipe from one pocket and a tin of loose tobacco from another. Jolene watched as he stuffed the pipe, then struck a match and drew four sharp breaths until the rich, dark tobacco was smouldering. A strong, acrid aroma wafted through the air. Andrew inhaled.

Jolene studied the young soldier. He had decided to risk his life in the war. He must have, she thought, known his values and priorities and had the courage and conviction to act on that knowledge.

"Andrew came from Calgary, although he grew up in Halifax and his sister's still here," the major explained.

"We've just come from Calgary ourselves," offered Grandpa.

Andrew turned his head towards Grandpa, but his blue, near-transparent eyes did not follow. Jolene shivered. There was something strange about the young soldier.

"You don't say so." The major inhaled deeply on the smooth mouthpiece of the pipe. "Ypres," he repeated, releasing a steady stream of pale grey smoke through his nostrils. Jolene leaned forward, recognizing the sound of a story engraved in memory.

"Trench warfare." The major paused. "Miles of trenches along the front. Day after day the boys crouched in those narrow, sodden, muddy ditches, scrabbling with their hands to dig in, trying to keep their feet from rotting from trench foot." He exhaled another stubby column of smoke. "Rats scavenging on corpses, and lice everywhere."

A wave of nausea overcame Jolene and she turned dizzily away, but the major didn't seem to notice. "The air was alive with fragments of flying metal and exploding shells that turned comrades into corpses." He took a long drag on his pipe while Jolene took a deep breath of fresh air. Grandpa's hand found hers and gave it a gentle squeeze.

The major's eyes fixed on a point in the air somewhere past Jolene's head. "Then came the gas."

A vivid image of the gas mask exhibit at the Army Museum in the Citadel filled Jolene's mind. She braced herself for the major's words, not wanting to hear them, but feeling compelled to listen.

"It was a fine April day — warm, sunny and still. Late in the afternoon, a soft breeze started to blow and around four o'clock the German attack began. At first, it was the usual thing — rifle fire, the toc-toc-toc of machine guns and the shells bursting around us. But an hour later, we saw for the very first time the yellowish-green cloud creep low from the German lines across no-man's land towards our trenches." He paused and his silence weighed down the air. "Like an unearthly monster, it reached out strangling the men. Those in its path fell, gasping for air, choking and suffocating. And behind the green monster came the Germans, equipped with respirators. Our orders were to stay and fight and those who could, did — bayonets flashing in the growing darkness until they collapsed, exhausted and dizzy from the gas."

"Why did they stay?" asked Jolene, surprised by her own question.

Major Thurman held the stem of the pipe between his teeth. "It was war," he said simply. "In war, soldiers follow orders. If they didn't, it would be total chaos."

Jolene's throat felt dry and rough. Of course, soldiers had to follow orders, but nobody had ever used gas in battle before. Even the people giving those orders couldn't have understood what they were subjecting the soldiers to.

Major Thurman nodded towards the young soldier whose eyes were turned upwards towards the sky. "Andrew lost his sight and was sent home to the care of his sister."

Jolene's eyes darted to Andrew's transparent gaze. He was blind! Blinded by the chlorine gas that the Germans had used in the war.

The major patted Andrew's forearm. "Spared him from some other gruesome sights in battle, mind you." He held up his right hand.

Jolene squirmed beside Grandpa, wondering if Andrew would still have enlisted if he had known the results of that decision. She regarded Major Thurman. Would he have issued those orders that left Andrew blind and hundreds of others dead if he had known the consequences?

Major Thurman noticed her discomfort. "But such tales are not for these sunny days." He exhaled a cloud of smoke and waved his pipe in the direction of the hillside. "This is a favourite place for children. You see them tobogganing once the snow comes, flying kites on windy days and playing games year-round." He shaded his eyes and looked across the open field. "I bet there's a game happening that you could get in on right now."

Grandpa ruffled Jolene's hair. "Go check it out if you wish," he said. "Shall I meet you back here, say in an hour and a half?"

Jolene couldn't believe what she'd just heard. For the next ninety minutes she was completely free to roam an unknown city. "It's quite safe," said her grandfather, reading her mind, "but stay in the neighbourhood and use your head."

Jolene grinned at him. "I will," she promised. And then she was off, running across the open field, trying to shake off the major's horrible images of war.

A group of children was assembled at the base of a large tree. Jolene slowed as she approached them. A few of them were as tall as she was, but there were lots of younger ones, too. Some milled about slapping at the tree trunk while others rushed over the bank of the hill out of sight. Jolene waded down a gentle incline between bare-branched bushes and tall clumps of dying grass into a small clearing. Twigs caught on her coat and for a moment she wished that she could shed it. In the clearing out of the wind, the sun was warm and soothing. Her skirt swished around her knees and her petticoat caught on a thorny rose bush. She bent to untangle it and let out a gasp.

There, just off to her left at the edge of the clearing, lay the body of a little girl. Jolene's heart raced then slowed as the child's hand twitched. Nestled beside her was a small speckled grey and white dog. The child's body was curved around its furry back and her face, covered by fine, blonde curly hair, rested just above its droopy ears. The dog opened one dark eye and regarded Jolene suspiciously, but did not move as if it did not wish to disturb the child's sleep. Jolene watched the rhythmic rise and fall of the little girl's chest beneath the red braided trim of her navy dress. The dog's tail wagged, rustling the grasses. The child shifted, her head rolling away from the animal in her peaceful slumber. Long reddish-blond eyelashes curled upwards towards faint eyebrows. Fascinated, Jolene studied the beautiful child's creamy skin and pale pink lips. She looked, thought Jolene, like an angel might.

The dog perked up its ears and in the distance Jolene heard a voice calling. "Missy! Missy! Where are you, Little Miss?" She stepped back into the bushes just as a girl about her own age and height burst into the clearing. Jolene stared at her. She was the same striking image as the child except that she was dark and the little girl was fair. The girl's concerned blue eyes met her own, then darted towards the child. A smile lit up the newcomer's face, transforming her look of concern into one of amusement.

It was contagious and soon they were both giggling. Even the dog looked up with smiling eyes. "Were you calling the dog?" Jolene asked the girl in a whisper.

Laughter splintered the sunshine. The child's chin dropped onto her shoulder, but she did not awaken. "No," said the girl, reaching back to corral the waves of glossy hair that tumbled about her shoulders and readjusting her hat, which was similar to Jolene's. "Missy is my sister."

Jolene blushed. She didn't suppose that mistaking someone's sister for her dog made a very good first impression. "Sorry," she whispered helplessly.

The dark-haired girl giggled. She fiddled with one of the black buttons on the front of her coat. "Don't apologize," she said in a half-whisper. "I think it's funny."

The child stirred again, her hand reaching absently towards the dog. Again Jolene was reminded of the pictures she'd seen of tiny angels. "She looks like an angel."

"She almost was one." The older girl caught the folds of her skirt and twisted them. "When she was three, she got scarlet fever," she explained. "The night my baby sister died, the doctor said she would, too." She released her skirt and spread her arms wide in a gesture of not understanding. "But she didn't." She squatted beside the child, brushing a blonde ringlet off her cheek. "She's better now, although she still sleeps a lot."

Jolene was moved by the look of concern on the girl's face. "Her name is Missy?" she asked.

The dark-haired girl nodded and gently pulled another strand of hair from her sister's face. Her affection for the child was so obvious and powerful that Jolene could not take her eyes from them. The little girl stretched. Her eyelids quivered, but remained closed. "She had to stay in bed while she was recuperating and every day, after school, I'd go in for a visit. One day, she announced that the doctor had told her that she was the most important person in the house and that we were all to treat her that way. She insisted on being called Miss Martha." She paused. "Martha's her real name, but it never suited her anyway."

Jolene had to agree.

"So we started calling her Miss Martha, but it soon changed to Missy or Little Miss and it stuck."

At the mention of her name, the little girl opened her eyes. They were the colour of dark chocolate and speckled with flecks of gold. Jolene caught her breath. Maybe she was an angel.

"Oh no!" Missy exclaimed, her bottom lip dropping into a beautiful pout. "You found me, Cassie."

Cassie swept her sister up in her arms and hugged her. Jolene felt envious of their closeness.

"And now you have to be *it* because you were the last one found," announced Cassie. Beside them, the dog leaped for attention.

"Maybe not," said Missy. "Have you found her yet?" She pointed at Jolene who could do nothing but laugh. "Who is she anyway?" the little girl asked her sister, as if Jolene did not actually exist. Cassie set her sister down and shook the dead grass from the coat upon which Missy had been lying.

"I'm Jolene," said Jolene bending down to Missy's level.

Missy stuck out a delicate hand. "Missy," she said simply.

Jolene shook her hand. "Did you have a nice sleep?"

The little girl thought for a moment. "Yes," she declared finally, "I did." She looked up at Jolene. "I don't remember you," she said, her nose scrunching up in thought.

Jolene straightened up and regarded Cassie. "That's because I just arrived in Halifax yesterday."

"Really?" Cassie's voice was alive and intrigued. Jolene was struck by the energy that emanated from her. "Where did you come from?"

"From Calgary," she replied, and then, noticing Missy's confused expression, added, "a city in the west."

Cassie's blue eyes brimmed with excitement. "That must have been a long train ride," she said enviously. "I've never been on a train."

"They're fun," said Jolene, remembering the old-fashioned steam train she'd ridden at Heritage Park. "But I'm glad I'm here now."

"How long are you staying?" asked Missy, slipping her coat on and tucking her hat into her pocket before leading the way up the small bushy incline.

"Just a few days." The astonished look on Cassie's face made Jolene add, "My mom is here for some meetings at the university." She bit her bottom lip, wondering if the university even existed in 1917.

But there was no reason to be alarmed. "For the war, I bet," said Cassie quickly. "I don't suppose you're allowed to talk about it either."

"Uh, not really," stammered Jolene. She followed Cassie and Missy out into the open field. The children who had been playing hide-and-seek were now racing about on the other side of the plateau.

"And that means that you probably haven't seen any of Richmond yet." Cassie clicked her tongue thoughtfully. "Where are you staying?"

"On Kaye Street," replied Jolene. They had stopped next to the bushes. The dog stood beside Missy and her fingers rarely left its back.

Cassie glanced towards the noisy children. "Why don't we take Missy home and then I can show you around?" she offered.

Missy looked up with a slight frown. "All right," she agreed reluctantly. "I want to go see the kittens anyway."

"Kittens?" The word escaped from Jolene's mouth before she'd thought about it.

"Missy's got this way with animals," explained Cassie as they headed down the hill on a dirt path between the bushes. Jolene glanced back at the bench where Grandpa, Major Thurman and Andrew were still sitting. She had a good hour to explore.

"Our cat, Cat, had kittens about five weeks ago, but she won't let them out of the shed yet, not even to show me," said Missy, as if the thought was utterly incomprehensible. "I know there's at least two of them, but they make enough noise for seven."

Jolene grinned. She fell into step beside Cassie with Missy and the dog tucked between them. Missy rambled on happily as Jolene took in her new surroundings. She could see, hear and smell the ocean at the bottom of the hill.

"Look out! Runaway bicycles!" screamed a voice behind them. They whirled around to see three boys on bicycles barrelling down the hill towards them.

"Out of control!" yelled another voice as the bicycle closest to them picked up speed on the incline. The boy riding it waved his arms wildly in the girls' direction, his legs sticking straight out to the sides, his pedals spinning.

"Quick!" breathed Cassie, grabbing Missy's hand. She pulled her little sister towards the bushes that lined the path, while Jolene scurried after them, the bicycles rapidly approaching.

"Watch out!"

Standing well off the trail, Jolene looked back up the hill. The riders had changed course and were steering straight for them. "What are they doing?" she gasped as she, Cassie and Missy pressed themselves against the branches.

"I can't stop!" shrieked one of the boys, now only metres from plowing into them. Jolene could see his excited eyes and open mouth. He was riding straight at her. Her heart hammering, she leaped into the thicket, half-expecting the bicycle and its rider to crash into it behind her. A wave of wind swept past her as the riders flew past, narrowly avoiding the bushes and hurling laughter into the sky.

Beside her, she heard Missy moan. Jolene struggled to her feet, pulling branches from her skirt and twigs from her hair. In a nearby bush, she located her hat, as well as Cassie and Missy, covered in leaves and scratches. "Who was that?" asked Jolene, helping Missy up.

"My brother," replied Cassie through clenched teeth, "and his stupid friends."

Jolene dusted off Missy's coat as Cassie joined them, a bloody scratch on her left temple. "Are they always like that?" Jolene asked.

"They're boys!" said Missy as if that explained everything.

"And they're in trouble with Ma!" added her sister.

Missy whistled for the dog who was still barking at the trail of dust the bicycles had left behind. Together, they resumed walking down the dirt path, occasionally plucking a twig from each other's hair.

"This is Roome Street," announced Cassie as the path widened into a road. A large, treed park bordered one side of the street. On the opposite side was a two-storey home with chocolate-coloured shutters. A tiny woman with a long pointed nose stood in its doorway and waved at the girls as they passed.

"And that's our neighbour, Mrs. Noseworthy," Missy informed her in a serious tone. Jolene stifled a laugh. "Ma says she's a very knowledgeable woman and that she's worthy of her name."

Cassie giggled. "That's because she always has her nose in everybody else's business." But she returned the woman's greeting.

"Here we are," announced Cassie, two houses later. "This is our place." They had stopped in front of a white wooden house with a large, dirty front window.

Missy darted around the side of the house, tugging at Jolene's hand. In the cluttered backyard, a small shack leaned to one side. Missy squatted in front of it and peered into a sort of tunnel that ran the length of the shed. Immediately, a ginger-coloured cat with white patches emerged and rubbed up against the little girl. "Hello Cat," Missy said. "May we see your kittens today, please?" The cat sat back on her haunches, meowed loudly and began to lick her paw. Jolene could see that she was still nursing. "All right," replied Missy, "but you will show them to me when you're ready, won't you?" Cat tilted her head to one side and purred.

Missy squinted into the tunnel. "If you look carefully, you might see them," she told Jolene. "I think they're sleeping."

Jolene could just make out the balls of orange fluff. "They're still so little." She longed to hold one of the tiny creatures.

"Maybe you can have one when they're old enough to go to other homes," suggested Missy.

Jolene's heart skipped a beat. If only she could get Michael to agree.

"Come on, Cat," said Missy matter-of-factly. "I'm sure we

can find you some milk." She disappeared inside the back door of the house as a tall, gangly boy stepped out. Jolene recognized him as one of the reckless bicyclists.

"Hi Cass," he said, looking curiously at Jolene. "Who's this?"

"This is Jolene," Cassie replied. "Jolene, this is my brother, Reg. He tried to run you over on the hill."

"Uh, hi," muttered Jolene.

Reg snickered. "You looked terrified," he told the girls. "It was so funny."

"I doubt if Ma will think so," said Cassie.

Her brother pulled a woolen cap over his dark hair and grabbed the handlebars of a rusty bicycle that was propped against the house. "You won't tell."

Jolene braced herself for Cassie's retort, but none came.

Instead, Reg wheeled his bicycle towards them. "Where are you going?" Cassie demanded.

"To the talking pictures at the Empire Theatre."

Cassie scowled. "That's your money for Christmas presents," she reminded him.

Reg straddled the bicycle and laughed. "Then I guess you won't get one." He pushed himself onto the seat and unbuttoned his jacket.

"Brothers!" muttered Cassie.

Jolene chuckled. "I know," she said. "I have one, too."

Reg stood with his toes touching the ground on either side of the bike. "Are you staying home now, Cass?" he asked, his voice suddenly serious.

"I was planning on showing Jolene around," said Cassie, but her voice had also softened. "Why, is she not having a good day?"

Reg shrugged. "She's sleeping now and so is Ben." He rolled past them. "Missy's here, so it's probably okay, but don't be too long." And then he was gone.

"My mother," explained Cassie, "isn't well." Her voice was sad, her blue eyes cloudy. "Three weeks ago we received a telegram. My eldest brother, James, was killed in the battle at Passchendaele."

"I, I'm sorry," stammered Jolene. It was no wonder she hadn't told on Reg.

"Mmm," murmured Cassie. "Ever since then, Ma hasn't been herself." Her delicate fingers disappeared into the folds of her skirt. "It was hard for all of us. He was just eighteen, you know, but Ma's taking it real bad. It's like she's gone somewhere and isn't coming back."

Jolene closed her eyes against Cassie's pain. "Maybe things will get better with time," she said, trying to sound hopeful.

"Maybe." Cassie didn't sound convinced. "But it wasn't like this when we lost Grandma or even when the baby died of scarlet fever." She stared at the cold earth.

Jolene wrestled with her thoughts. It couldn't be easy to lose a parent or a child, no matter what the circumstances were. And yet, death in old age or illness was a natural part of life. There was nothing natural about death in war. She reached out and squeezed Cassie's hand.

Chapter Six

"Have you lost anyone in the war?" Cassie asked, as they made their way around to the front of the house and back onto Roome Street. Jolene shook her head. "You're lucky." Cassie pointed at a small house half-hidden by trees. "The Marshalls lost two sons, and the Reynolds," she said indicating a house down the street, "lost their father and uncle. One of the boys at my school lost three brothers, his father and two cousins." A sigh escaped from deep within her. "So many men have already died and who knows how many more will die before it ends."

Listening to Cassie's words, Jolene realized how much the war had shaped her new friend's character. Like her neighbours and the rest of her family, Cassie had had to cope in the face of tragedy and threat. In her short lifetime, she had dealt with so much and it had given her a depth and maturity that Jolene couldn't help noticing. Had it also helped her understand who she was and what she stood for? Jolene tried to remember what she'd heard about World War One. "It'll be over soon," she said, recalling that it had ended on November 11, 1918.

"That's what they said when it started. That it would be over in a few months' time. That our soldiers would be home by Christmas." Cassie fell silent. "That was more than three years ago."

They crossed the street to the park and Cassie suddenly raced forward, as if she could outrun her uncomfortable memories. Jolene sprinted after her. "This is Mulgrave Park," Cassie said, twirling around when she reached the middle. "We run through it everyday on our way to school, even though it's not really on our way." She stopped halfway through a twirl. "Do you think you might stay until Christmas?"

Jolene shook her head.

"That's too bad." Cassie pulled her hat from her head. "If you were going to, you could audition for a part in the Christmas play at church." Together they raced the rest of the way across the park. "When I'm older, I want to act in those talking pictures," said Cassie. The wind gusted, whipping her long hair dramatically across her face.

Jolene could almost imagine Cassie's beautiful dark features on the screen. "Did you audition for the Christmas play this year?"

Cassie nodded. "Oh yes, and I can have the lead if I can

come to all the rehearsals." Her voice fell flat. "But now with Ma being the way she is and Beth married and pregnant, so many of the chores fall to me. Some days I can't even get to school, never mind stop at the church hall afterwards for rehearsal."

Jolene watched her sympathetically. "Who's Beth?" she asked as Cassie turned in the direction of the harbour.

"Beth is my older sister. She and Rory live in the upper flat of the Morrisons' place and she comes by to help fairly often. But now that she's expecting a baby in March, she needs to rest more."

They stopped at a wide cobblestone street as a tram rattled by. The street was full of wagons and motorcars and soldiers in uniform. "This is Campbell Road," announced Cassie as a ship's whistle blew in the distance.

She skipped a few steps, a smile leaping to her lips. "Beth's husband Rory is this giant of a man with a Scottish accent and Beth's such a tiny little thing. You should have seen the way he courted her. It was so romantic." She let out a long, dreamy breath. "He was with the 85th Battalion, the Cape Breton Highlanders, and he was posted to Halifax before going overseas. One Sunday, a year ago last fall, we were all in the Public Gardens and Rory was there with a group from his battalion. There are so many soldiers in Halifax now," she added.

"Well, there was a duck there and it had got its head hooped through some wire. It stumbled around trying to fly, trying to get untangled, but it was hopeless. One of the soldiers noticed it first and a few of the men were troubling the poor creature, playing with the end of the wire and sending it into fits." She frowned, remembering. "If there's one thing Beth can't stand it's when a living creature is mistreated. She marched right into the midst of those soldiers, our tiny Beth did, and told them all to stop being cruel and heartless. Then she walked over to the duck, scooped it up and eased its head out of the hoop of wire. A couple of the men snickered, but not Rory. He walked up to Beth, dropped to one knee and proclaimed that any woman capable of such love for a duck must surely be able to love a man better." Cassie giggled. "He claims he fell in love with her right then and there. That he knew she was the only woman he could ever love."

Jolene sighed. "That's so romantic."

"Married her two days before his battalion set sail on the *Olympic*. She was awfully upset about his going. But he told her that nothing, not even the Germans, could keep him from returning to her."

"And he came back?"

"He came home last June after a bayonet sliced his shoulder. But he's healing up pretty well." Cassie grinned. "Beth's so happy, although she tries not to let on so much — especially around Ma because of James and all."

Jolene watched Cassie closely. It was so complicated to live during World War I, where tragedy, death and loss were a way of life.

The blast of a train made her look up. They had arrived

at a railyard where black locomotives shunted back and forth on the tracks. Men scurried about everywhere and the smell of burning coal filled the air.

"This is the Richmond Railyard," said Cassie, climbing the stairs to an iron pedestrian bridge that crossed the railway tracks. "My father works here."

Jolene heard the clickety-clack of the wheels on the track as a locomotive huffed and puffed towards them, uncoupling a few cars. "Look, there's a man standing on top of that boxcar," shouted Jolene.

"That's the brakeman. That's what my father does." The man was bundled in a heavy overcoat. He wore gloves and a peaked hat pulled low over his face. The shunting car he was riding slowed and then coupled to a line of cars ahead with a thud. Soot and cinders rained down on him.

"Isn't it dangerous?" asked Jolene.

"Sometimes. Ma calls it the widow-maker job and occasionally a brakeman does slip and get run over, but my father loves it. He rides the trains out of the city to the Rockingham Railyards and brings back freight cars," explained Cassie. "Then the freight handlers unload them and the stevedores load the goods onto the ships to take overseas. Rory is a security guard at one of the shipping wharves and two of my uncles are stevedores."

Jolene marvelled at the size and closeness of Cassie's family. Aside from Grandpa, her closest relatives lived in Vancouver. She thought she heard a horse neigh, but could see nothing except smoke and tracks and a churning loco-motive as it passed beneath her. Then she heard it again. "That sounded like a horse."

"I heard they were taking a shipload of horses to the west-ern front." Cassie shaded her eyes with one hand. "I wonder if they know that they're going to war?"

"I doubt it," said Jolene. "But it's not like they have a choice."

"Will your brother go when he's old enough?"

Jolene gagged and coughed. "He's too young," she man-aged finally.

"So is Reg, but he's aching to go and fight when he's able to. Besides, with conscription now, they'll have to enlist when they're eighteen."

"The war will be over long before then," said Jolene know-ingly.

Cassie studied her face. "I hope you're right," she said finally.

They jumped down off the pedestrian bridge and made their way back up the steep hill. "There's my school." Cassie pointed ahead at a large, two-storey stone structure with a face of windows. "I'm in grade seven, but we share a class-room with the grade eights and nines, including Reg."

"I know what that's like," said Jolene half-laughing. "Mi-chael's been in my class every year since we started school."

"Really? You must have a very small school." Cassie tugged her hat back on and tilted it over her left eye.

"Not exactly," said Jolene. "It's just that we're twins."

"Twins?" Surprised eyes scrutinized Jolene's face. "Is that the truth?"

"Absolutely," Jolene assured her. "We're not identical twins, of course."

"But you look alike?" A light shone in Cassie's eyes.

"Pretty much. Only Michael's a little taller."

"Is he older?"

"No, I am, by two minutes." She thought for a minute, then added, "And I act older — usually."

"Girls are always more mature than boys at our age. Ma says that's just the way we develop." Cassie sprang up onto a large boulder. "I've always wondered how it would be to have a twin." She beamed at Jolene. "What's it like?"

"Well," Jolene began thoughtfully, "sometimes it's a real pain." The glow in Cassie's eyes dimmed. "You know what brothers are like, how embarrassing they can be."

A sympathetic smile appeared on Cassie's lips. "Yes, but don't you have a special bond with your brother? Don't you know what he's going to say before he speaks? Don't you see the world the same way?"

"Sometimes," admitted Jolene. "Last year at school, our teacher gave us this assignment where we had to imagine the reaction of someone from another planet if they came to our city."

Cassie giggled. "Our teachers aren't that imaginative."

Realizing how silly the idea of space travel must seem in 1917, Jolene hurriedly continued. "Michael and I did our assignments completely on our own. He was away." She stopped short of saying that he'd been at a swim meet in Edmonton. "And I was at home. When we handed them in, the teacher called us up and asked who had copied whom. They were almost exactly alike."

"See!" exclaimed Cassie. "It must be so wonderful to be a twin. How else are you alike?"

"Well, we're both pretty athletic. Michael's a swimmer," Jolene said, choosing her words carefully, "and I like to do tumbling." She didn't explain that she spent five days a week training for competitive gymnastics.

"You mean like the trapeze artists at the circus?" Cassie's voice was breathless.

Jolene chewed on a smile. "Sort of."

"Can you do a back flip?"

Jolene nodded. Her back layout was one of the best in the club. "But not in my skirt," she added, looking down at the bulky folds of material.

Cassie's eyes sparkled. "Maybe one day," she said, gazing at the clear sky, "you'll be a great trapeze artist. You'll travel throughout the world with the circus and perform dangerous tricks high above wide-eyed audiences."

Jolene stifled a laugh. It wasn't exactly what she dreamed of and she was pretty sure her parents would object, but there was something infectious about Cassie's enthusiasm. "And you'll be a famous actress touring the world to visit your fans and appearing on the silver screen."

"In romantic love stories and tragic dramas." Cassie's eyes

were wide and blue like the sapphire in Jolene's mother's ring. "And some times we'll be together, in the same place, like we are now."

"England, France, Spain, Switzerland . . ."

"But not Germany," Cassie added quickly. "We won't go to Germany."

"No," agreed Jolene, remembering the times.

"And we'll stay in luxurious hotel suites with hot bubble baths and soft divans where we'll lounge all day. . ."

"Listening to exquisite music and eating scrumptious chocolates."

"And men will bring us gifts," continued Cassie, stretching her elegant fingers towards Jolene.

"Diamonds and rubies and tiaras that will litter our dressers. And long-stemmed red roses . . ."

"In winter."

Jolene caught her breath, riveted by the aura that surrounded Cassie, the dream sparkling in her eyes. Maybe dreaming was one way of coping. Cassie's eyes flickered towards hers and a giggle burst from her lips. Jolene snickered then laughed as Cassie threw her arms around her in a sudden hug. "Oh, it will be so grand, Jolene. Just wait until they see us — Michael and Reg and Beth and Rory and our parents. Ma once dreamed of being a singer you know, but then . . ." Her voice trailed off. "I'd better get back and tend to Ma," she said quietly, the light in her eyes abruptly extinguished by her reality.

Jolene nodded, reluctant to leave, but anxious about how

long it had been since she'd left Grandpa. "I should be getting back, too." They walked to the corner together. Fort Needham lay at the top of the hill and Cassie's home below. "Maybe I'll see you again," said Jolene as they reached the street.

"Why don't you come to Point Pleasant Park with us tomorrow?" Cassie's eyes shone. "It's out on the point by the ocean, but you can take the tram. We often go on a Sunday and we're sure to go tomorrow if the weather holds. Please," she pleaded. "Then you can meet Beth and Rory, too."

"That would be great," said Jolene. "Mom and Dad might be busy, but I'll see if my grandfather will come."

"Promise?" Cassie squeezed Jolene's hand.

"Promise," said Jolene, gazing into the eyes of her new friend.

Cassie let her hand go. "I'll see you tomorrow," she cried, running in the direction of her house. "And bring your brother. I can't wait to meet your twin."

Jolene called goodbye and ran to find Grandpa. Should she bring Michael? She could introduce him to Cassie and Missy and Reg. She could just imagine his face when she and Grandpa told him that they'd found a way to travel back in time. Her feet slowed. But what if he said something he shouldn't or embarrassed her in front of her new friends? And that would mean sharing her and Grandpa's secret of time travelling. A whistle hooted in the harbour, filling her with doubt.

Grandpa waved at her from the bench, exactly where

she'd left him. She loped towards him. Major Thurman and Andrew had gone, but they'd left behind their newspaper. Jolene peered at the front page of *The Morning Chronicle*. A list of names of war casualties took up one column, a description of a battle another. She caught sight of a picture of soldiers debarking from a boat in the harbour before Grandpa picked up the paper. "Germans in Rags and Old Clothes" read one headline. The war was everywhere. It was no wonder that Cassie's mother had been enveloped by despair.

"It was a terrible war, wasn't it?" observed Jolene thoughtfully.

"Millions of men died in deplorable conditions while fighting over a hundred-mile front in a tiny northeast corner of France."

"Was it worth it?" asked Jolene cautiously.

Grandpa shrugged. "There are lots of Canadians who would say it wasn't, especially in the present looking back. But on the other hand, without our troops, the Germans might have won the war. Then everything would have been different."

Only hours earlier, Jolene had admired Andrew's conviction to fight. But since then, she had seen and heard the horrors and tragedies that went along with that decision. How did anyone make sense out of all these conflicting emotions? "There's no right answer, is there?"

Grandpa sighed. "No," he admitted. "Most of the important things in life are like that. What matters is that you think things through and decide what the right answer is for you based on your own values." He folded the paper in quarters and stuffed it into his jacket pocket, glancing one last time at the headlines. "The Great War," he murmured.

"Why did they call it that?"

They started towards the crest of the hill. "It was supposed to be the war to end all wars, Jo," he said sadly. "Little did they know that an even greater one was still to come."

World War Two. In just over two decades, warring forces would again slaughter thousands of soldiers and civilians. Would the world learn nothing from World War One? Jolene walked thoughtfully beside her grandfather. For a second time in their lifetimes, Cassie and her siblings would have to endure more wartime chaos and tragedy. That chaos and tragedy would inevitably destroy Cassie's dreams. How could it not? A house obscured the sun, partially shading their path. Jolene stepped into the sunshine, out of the long cold shadows of war.

Three blasts of a ship's whistle caught her attention and three shrill whistles responded. Jolene glanced back at the busy harbour. But first Cassie had to survive the Halifax explosion.

They walked in silence until they reached the time crease beside the church. Children called and a puppy barked from a doorway. "I think we can probably borrow these clothes for a few days," said Grandpa.

"Can we come back tomorrow?" asked Jolene. "I met this girl Cassie who wants to be an actress and she invited me to Point Pleasant Park. Her family goes out there most Sundays when the weather's nice."

Grandpa stopped walking as the words tumbled out of his granddaughter. "Your father has meetings scheduled tomorrow and your mother will be at the university. I told them I'd look after you and Michael."

Jolene dug the toe of her boot into the frozen dirt. "Really?" Confusion tore at her insides.

"You can't come alone," said Grandpa. "You promised that you would only come back with me."

Jolene hesitated. On one hand, she wasn't sure that she was ready to share all this with Michael. But if she didn't, then she wouldn't be able to go to Point Pleasant Park or see Cassie.

"Why are you so reluctant to bring Michael?"

Jolene shrugged. "It's hard to be your own person when you're a twin."

"But why? You two are as different on the inside as you are alike on the outside."

Jolene twirled her hair around two fingers. "I know and that's part of the problem."

Grandpa leaned against the wall of the church and waited.

"We look alike and so everyone expects us to be alike and we're not."

"You have some common traits. You're both kind and generous and tolerant of your old grandfather."

Jolene kicked at the frozen earth. "Michael's so energetic and talkative and fun." She cringed at the bitter undertone in her words.

"And you're a leader and kind and full of wonderfully innovative ideas," added Grandpa. "You have all kinds of special qualities."

"But nobody notices those things when Michael's around," she said, admitting aloud what she had only ever admitted to herself. "My special traits aren't so visible."

"Maybe at first," said Grandpa, "but they are in the end." He lifted her chin with two weathered fingers. "Didn't you just tell me that you want to be your own person?" Jolene nodded. "Would you want to be Michael?"

"No," admitted Jolene, half a grin curling one side of her mouth upwards. "I like to think before I speak."

Grandpa chuckled. "He does have a tendency to be impulsive."

"And he does some immature things sometimes."

"Occasionally," agreed Grandpa, smiling at her. "But even if you can live temporarily in 1917 not being a twin, you can't do it in the present." Grandpa twirled his moustache. "But it's your decision. If you want to keep this our secret for now, we can. But then we can't come back tomorrow."

Jolene contemplated Grandpa's words. It would be nice not to be a twin for a while. On the other hand, she'd been a twin all her life and she'd be a twin for the rest of her life. And Cassie had specifically asked her to bring her brother. It would be fun for her to meet him, even though Michael would probably be more interested in Reg and his friends. "He can come, Gramps. I guess he's always going to be a part of my life in some way or other."

Grandpa arched his eyebrows. "Let's hope so," he said before disappearing into the church lobby. He emerged a few moments later with a handful of boys' clothes. "These should do. Now, are you ready?"

Jolene retrieved her flip-flops from their hiding place. Stepping into the dense shadow, she felt the darkness grow warm and tingling and a hot breeze envelop her.

Chapter Seven

Jolene woke to the sound of Grandpa closing the door behind him. "What time is it?" she asked, stretching. "And where have you been, Gramps?"

"It's almost 10:30 and I've been for a walk in the neighbourhood."

"The 1917 neighbourhood?" she whispered, eyeing Michael's closed door.

Grandpa shook his head. "Not yet."

Jolene bounced off the pullout. "So can we go?"

"Once Michael's up."

"Oh yeah," she groaned, wondering if she'd made the right decision yesterday. "He's never going to believe you when you tell him about the time creases."

"Why not?" asked Grandpa. "You did."

"Not right away. Initially I thought you were crazy." She smiled at him. "Michael will too."

"I'm not so sure," Grandpa said. "Michael has complete trust in certain people." He looked pointedly at Jolene.

"We'll see," she murmured, slipping out the front door. Yesterday, when they had returned, they had stashed their borrowed clothes inside the wooden bench on the front porch. Jolene returned with a large pile of garments. Grandpa's newspaper, dated December 1, 1917, was still in his jacket pocket. "At least we have your newspaper as proof."

"Proof of what?" Michael stumbled into the living room as Jolene threw the garments into the front hall closet and closed the door.

"We'll tell you after my shower," she said, disappearing into the washroom.

Jolene rinsed the last of her dishes and glanced at the clock. It was nearly noon. Cassie's family would probably already be at Point Pleasant Park. Michael had showered and was dawdling over his cereal. Grandpa was obviously waiting for him to finish. Jolene cleared her throat twice and looked encouragingly at Grandpa.

"Michael," he said, "we have something to tell you." Michael looked up expectantly. "Years ago, your great-great-grandfather, who was a physicist, discovered some rather interesting information about energy and time. I found his journal."

Michael looked perplexed. He slurped on a spoonful of milk.

"He discovered that time is continuous, kind of like a long ribbon. The moments run into each other rather than one ending and another beginning. That means that any specific instant on the continuum has the properties of the continuum itself."

Michael's brow wrinkled and his eyes narrowed. "I don't get it."

Grandpa scratched his temple. "Basically, he discovered that the past, present and future are not really separate times — they're all one."

Michael swirled the milk in his bowl as Grandpa continued. "But energy isn't continuous. And sometimes when there's lots of energy in a place, it gets trapped in the time continuum."

"So why was that such an important discovery?"

"Because that trapped energy forms a time crease — kind of like a crease in a ribbon."

"A time crease?"

Jolene fidgeted. It wasn't easy to explain a time crease and it was even harder to convince someone that they actually existed. If they didn't hurry up, she'd miss the whole day with Cassie at Point Pleasant Park. Leaving Grandpa to his explanation, she crossed the room and pulled open the closet door, searching for the 1917 newspaper.

"Time creases are hot shadows that you can slip through."

Grandpa paused for effect. "Into another time."

Michael looked skeptical. "You mean like time travel?"

Grandpa nodded.

Michael wiped his mouth with a napkin and raised his eyebrows. "You mean you've found a way to go back into the past or ahead into the future?"

Jolene rummaged for the newspaper, pulling clothes out of the closet. "Yes," said Grandpa simply.

"Get out!" Michael scraped his chair back. Jolene continued her search. The paper was just what they needed to convince him. "Really?"

"Really!" said Grandpa. "These time creases often occur at the site of disasters or events where there's lots of energy released. Jo and I went back into the town of Frank just days before the slide in 1903." He gestured towards Jolene who was still digging in the closet.

Michael's eyes darted to his sister.

"And yesterday, here in Halifax, we went back to 1917," continued Grandpa.

Silence fell over the room. "Jo?" Michael was on his feet, the question in his eyes and on his lips.

Jolene located the newspaper and pulled it out of the closet. "Really!" she said looking her brother square in the eyes and holding up the paper.

But there was no need for her proof. "Sweet!" Michael's face was bright with excitement. "You mean we can go back in time — here, now, today?"

"Yes," said Grandpa. "Back to 1917."

Jolene stood in the pile of clothing, marvelling at her brother's easy acceptance.

"Are those for me?" He darted across the room and pointed at the garments surrounding her.

"Just a minute, Michael," said Grandpa. "It's true that we can go back, but there are a few things you have to know." He cleared his throat. "First, not everyone can go through the time creases. We think you can because of your experience at the Citadel the other day. Those people dressed in filthy clothes weren't part of a re-enactment. They were the injured and homeless who actually came to the Citadel after the explosion."

"In 1917?"

"Yes. We were looking through a sort of window into history." Grandpa paused. "Your father can't see those windows or travel back in time, so it has to be our secret."

"That's too bad."

"And no matter what happens back there, you can't change history." Grandpa's expression was sad and serious. "Do you understand that? You can't change history."

Jolene nodded in solemn agreement. She had learned that last time, but it hadn't been an easy lesson.

"Okay," said Michael.

"And finally, you are not permitted to go back without me," added Grandpa. "Under no circumstances. Are you clear on that point?"

Michael nodded. "Sure," he said impatiently. "So what are we waiting for?"

Grandpa twirled his moustache. "You," he said, smiling.

"Here." Jolene handed her brother a pair of brown tweed trousers, a matching jacket, a worn shirt and a tweed cap. "Make sure you wear your hiking boots."

Michael almost leaped across the room. "1917!" he said incredulously as he ducked into his bedroom to change. By the time he'd emerged, both Grandpa and Jolene were dressed in their 1917 garments. "You look so cute in that hat," Michael told Jolene.

"Almost as cute as you," she replied, grinning at him. But she had to admit that the outfit and cap suited him.

Michael jammed his hands into his jacket pockets, posing. "Hey!" he said, pulling out a handkerchief and a handful of coins. "Money." Seven nickels and two pennies jingled in his hand.

"Better hang onto those," advised Grandpa. "Our loonies and toonies wouldn't go over very well in 1917."

"So how do you go through the time creases?" asked Michael as they made their way past some curious onlookers to the church.

"There are two ways to think of yourself in time," explained Grandpa. "Either you are travelling with time past a location, like a stick floating downstream, or you are situated in one location, letting time pass you by."

"Come on," called Jolene scrambling up the church steps

with Grandpa and Michael on her heels. "I'll show you." She stepped into the hot dense shadow. "One location in time," she muttered as the shade came alive. Michael's hand gripped her arm as a blast of hot air hit them. Catching her breath, she felt the trapped energy pulling and stretching her. The shade grew deeper and darker. She swayed and lost her balance as she was sucked forward into light. Jolene straightened up, breathing hard.

Beside her, Michael stood grasping the wall of the church, his chest heaving. "I couldn't breathe," he stammered. "It felt like my head was going to explode." Grandpa put a comforting hand on his shoulder and the panic in Michael's voice subsided. "It's all changed," he said looking around in awe.

"It's 1917," said Jolene. She turned to Grandpa. "Can we go to Point Pleasant Park, please? We can catch the tram."

"Point Pleasant Park," murmured Grandpa. "That's the one we could see from the Citadel." He glanced at Michael who was still taking everything in wide-eyed. "We'll need money for the tram."

Michael dug his coins out of his pocket. "How far can we go on thirty-seven cents?"

"Probably a lot farther than you think," said Grandpa. "Now that streetcar stop would be . . ."

"At the bottom of this hill," called Jolene charging down the hill. "Cassie and I saw it yesterday."

Michael raced after her. "Who's Cassie?"

"A friend of mine." Jolene stopped in her tracks and Michael almost collided with her. "And please don't embarrass me in front of her," she pleaded. "No stupid or gross stuff, okay? Just act mature."

Grandpa caught up with them at the corner of Campbell Road. Uniformed soldiers and sailors pushed past them. A wagon pulled by Clydesdales clattered by on the cobblestones, sharing the road with antique-looking motorcars. A horn sounded and the horses skittered sideways. "Easy," came the voice of the driver perched high on the driver's box.

"Wow!" exclaimed Michael. "I'd like to bring a Porsche here."

Grandpa raised his eyebrows. "Porsche is a German company. I'm not sure I'd advise it in the midst of the war."

Michael gasped. "You have to watch what you say, " advised Jolene. "And there's the tram."

A box-like streetcar with half a dozen cathedral-shaped windows on either side trundled down the street, its overhead cables flashing atop the power lines. They sprinted towards a group of people assembled at a nearby stop, paid a nickel for a ticket and clambered aboard. Grandpa sat beside a sailor with a crisp sailor's cap and Michael took the seat next to Jolene. They stared out the windows at the bustling shops advertising Christmas gifts: skates, spinning tops, slippers, fountain pens, gloves and silk stockings.

A ship's horn blared and Michael turned his attention to

the harbour where a troopship painted with black and white stripes running in all directions swung out into the water. "Why is it painted like that?" he asked.

The sailor beside Grandpa responded. "It's called a dazzle pattern and it's intended to confuse enemy submarines."

"Sweet!" breathed Michael before Jolene nudged him in the ribs with her elbow.

The tram squealed to a stop and Jolene stared at the shops and multi-storey brick buildings. Two posters adorned the window of a store. *Women of Britain say "Go!"* proclaimed the first one in which wives and mothers stood proudly watching soldiers march off to war. *"Daddy, what did YOU do in the great war?"* asked another. It depicted a small girl sitting on her father's lap, reading while a young boy played with toy soldiers. The man had an expression of regret on his face.

"What's that big building?" asked Michael, indicating a sprawling three-storey stone structure with a raised dome and clock.

"That's the North Street Railway Station," said the sailor. Wagons and motorcars milled about at the entrance as travellers spilled out of its splendid front doors. "It has a glass roof."

The tram continued onto Barrington Street through the downtown district of Halifax and into the south end. There, Jolene noticed, the houses were bigger, built of stone or brick with impressive bay windows. Frost had flattened the gardens and deadened the vines that grew from the secluded doorways, up and around the shuttered windows. Richmond, she realized, was home to the working poor.

"The next stop is ours," said Grandpa, thanking the sailor beside him. The air was salty and moist as they stepped off the tram. Bells clanged and buoys groaned. Grandpa led the way into Point Pleasant Park as a gentle mist rolled in off the sea.

Chapter Eight

A small beach ran along the edge of Point Pleasant Park towards a rocky point. Families dotted the beach and lawns. Men gathered in clumps on the edge of the trees and women, their dresses billowing in the wind, strolled up and down. Young lovers, holding hands, turned onto tree-lined paths or emerged laughing. Jolene watched as a young soldier in uniform chased after his girlfriend's wide-brimmed hat. He retrieved it and she pinned it back into her hair with a long pin. Michael wandered towards the ocean's edge.

"Jolene!" Cassie broke free from a group and raced towards her, the pompom on her hat bouncing wildly. Jolene met her in a joyous embrace. "I knew you'd come."

Grandpa joined them and Jolene turned to introduce them. "Cassie, this is my grandfather."

Grandpa smiled kindly. "Hello, Cassie." He winked at the girls. "I think I'll leave you young folk to your pleasures and find some old storytellers to amuse me."

"My father and uncles are just over by that stand of trees," said Cassie, pointing. "They love to tell stories."

"Thank you, young lady. So do I." Grandpa tipped his cap at her and ambled in the direction Cassie had indicated. Jolene smiled after him as Michael joined them.

"And you must be Jolene's twin brother." Cassie's eyes sparkled.

"Cassie, this is Michael," said Jolene, looking from her new friend to her brother.

Michael's eyes were riveted on Cassie's face. Colour crept up his cheeks. It took a moment before he found his voice. "Hello, Cassie. It's a pleasure to meet you." He removed his cap and inclined his head towards her, ignoring Jolene's shocked expression.

"The pleasure's mine," Cassie replied, with a mock curt-sey and an amused smile.

"It's Jolene, isn't it?" Reg had burst onto the scene and was addressing the girls.

"Michael," Cassie said, "this is my brother Reg."

Reg glanced from Michael to Jolene and back again. "You sure do look alike. Got the same eyes." Michael's eyes, Jolene noticed, were fixed on Cassie who had shyly diverted hers to the ground. She stood with her fingers entwined in the folds of her dress, swaying.

"We're twins," explained Jolene.

Reg nodded and looked out to sea. "There's a boat," he cried, racing in the direction of the point. Michael followed with long, athletic strides.

"He's just like you and just as I imagined him," said Cassie, giggling. "Attractive, strong and athletic." She hiked up her dress and ran after the boys. Jolene followed, wondering if Cassie's compliment was intended for her or Michael.

Jolene watched Michael leap onto a large boulder beside Reg. He had a swimmer's build — broad, powerful shoulders and a slim waist — but she'd never thought of him as handsome before.

"What is it?" asked Michael pointing at the distant boat.

Reg squinted into the sun. "It's a ferry." Jolene felt the low vibrations of a ship's horn in the pit of her stomach. "And there's a steamer."

The bow of a boat slid into view on the far side of McNab's Island. Reg jumped down from his rocky perch. "Come on," he called.

Michael sprinted after him, but Cassie took Jolene's hand and swung it happily. They strolled in the direction of their brothers. "We love it here," she told Jolene. "In the autumn, the maple leaves swirl to the ground like dancers in colourful skirts." Ahead of them Reg and Michael stooped to skim stones across the quiet waters of an inlet.

Cumulous clouds began to build over the point on the far side of the bay. Reg bent to pick something up and mo-

tioned excitedly to Michael who quickly joined him. Immediately, the two boys darted inland.

Jolene looked at Cassie whose eyes reflected her suspicion. Without a word, they chased after the boys, running
down a treed trail and stopping at a clearing scattered with
wood. A ring of blackened stones enclosed a small tipi of
branches and twigs. Reg stood poised above it, a burning
match in his hand. "Where did you get those?" demanded
Cassie as Reg lowered the match. The branches ignited and
crackled. A coil of smoke escaped.

"I found them," stated Reg. He dragged a larger piece of
wood towards the fire and threw it on. Michael added
another and Jolene felt a rush of heat.

She caught her brother's eye. Michael shrugged. They
weren't far from the water and others had obviously started
fires here before. As if the same thought had occurred to
Cassie, she seated herself on a nearby log. Jolene joined her
as Michael and Reg stacked more branches beside the shallow firepit.

"Bet you can't do this," challenged Reg. He leaped over
the knee-high flames as the girls let out a gasp.

"What? This?" demanded Michael, springing easily over
the pit.

Cassie and Jolene stared at their brothers.

Reg picked up another branch and hurled it on the fire.
Michael did the same. Light burst and flames roared. Cassie
shifted uneasily on the log beside Jolene, then shook her

head as Reg positioned himself a few paces from the pit. "Reg, don't! It's too high." Ignoring her protest, Reg took a short run and jumped. Flames reached for his shoes, but he landed safely on the other side, smiling broadly.

All eyes turned towards Michael. Jolene rose to her feet. The burning branches reached to the middle of her thigh. "Michael," she said with a sharp intake of breath, but her brother was already in the air, his long legs tucked beneath him. She heard his landing thud and exhaled.

Michael and Reg stood grinning at one another, the brightness of the fire illuminating their faces. Reg heaved a thick branch into the pit, spattering hot embers on the dirt. "I dare you," he challenged Michael as flames covered the log.

Tongues of red, yellow and orange darted as high as Jolene's waist. The reflection of the fire in Reg's eyes made him appear mad. "You're crazy!" she told Reg, her heart rate edging up a notch. "Michael, don't be an idiot."

Michael's eyes studied his sister's, then took in Cassie's frightened expression.

"It's too dangerous," she whispered.

Michael stepped backwards.

An image of a body, clothes on fire, twisting and writhing filled Jolene's mind. "Michael, please."

The wind gusted and the fire surged upwards. "It's too dangerous, man," Michael said, eyeing Reg.

Reg's laughter cackled above the flames. "You're scared," he taunted.

"Yep," confirmed Michael, "but I ain't stupid."

Cassie giggled and the tension in Jolene's shoulders eased.

But Reg was not easily deterred. He plucked at the buttons of his wool jacket and backed away from the blaze. "I can jump that."

"No!" screamed Cassie moving towards her brother who was already running towards the firepit. He launched himself into the air. His feet, tucked tightly into his body, disappeared inside a circle of flame, then re-emerged, stretching for the ground. Jolene heard one foot thud onto the dirt beside her, then saw the other one land and twist on a rough stone. Reg's arms circled wildly. With a desperate cry, he lost his balance and fell back into the flames.

Jolene lunged for his jacket, catching his collar as the stench of burning wool reached her. Reg swung sideways, then staggered away from the fire as she let go, fighting to keep her own balance. "Help!" he screamed, frantically trying to slap the flames on his back.

Cassie's feet were already in motion. She dodged her brother's flailing arms and grabbed for his buttons. "Get your coat off!"

"Water!" cried Michael, bolting down the path.

Jolene slapped at the flames spreading across Reg's jacket, her mind racing.

Reg twisted frantically away, knocking Cassie's hands. "I can't get the buttons undone," she cried.

Michael reappeared in the clearing. "I need a bucket."

Reg spun around, fanning the flames and backing up against the log the girls had been seated on. "Do something!" he shrieked.

Without warning, Jolene charged at him, knocking him over the log, flat onto his back.

"What are you doing?" screamed Cassie.

"Roll!" commanded Jolene.

"What?" Cassie's eyes were wide and crazed.

"It will smother the flames," explained Jolene. "Roll!"

Reg rolled back and forth in the dirt, then finally lay still. Cassie climbed over the log and knelt beside him. "Reg, are you okay?"

Slowly Reg sat up, tugged at a couple of stubborn buttons and removed his charred jacket. Only its thin lining separated the burnt material and his shirt. Cassie threw an arm around his heaving shoulders. "You burnt your hair," she said, holding up a frazzled strand.

Reg brushed her hand away. He pushed himself to his feet. "I could have made it if the wind hadn't gusted," he proclaimed, dusting himself off. "At least I had the guts to try."

Michael frowned but made no reply.

"We'd better put the fire out," suggested Jolene. "Can we use your jacket to haul sand?"

"Sure," said Reg. "I'm going to tell Ma I lost it."

Cassie's eyebrows arched but she did not reprimand her brother.

Together they extinguished the fire, sifting through the

ashes until not a single ember glowed. Then they headed back to the water's edge. Reg dug into his pocket and hurled his box of matches into the ocean.

Cassie stood beside Jolene, watching her brother. "He's such a fool," she said softly. "I love him so much." She smiled sheepishly at her friend. "Thank you."

Jolene could find no words to respond, but none seemed necessary. Side by side, they retraced their steps up the beach. Reg and Michael followed behind them. For what seemed like an eternity, they walked in silence.

"What's that?" asked Michael, restoring conversation and a sense of normalcy. He pointed to a boat anchored off McNab's Island in the mouth of the harbour.

"The examination boat," replied Cassie. "It checks every boat entering the harbour."

Reg pointed at another vessel heading their way. "There's the patrol boat. At dusk, they close the gates in the anti-submarine nets so that nothing can enter the harbour. They open them again each morning."

Michael looked confused. "There are German submarines here?"

Reg nodded solemnly. "I saw one last summer."

"You did not," scoffed Cassie. "The Germans aren't that close."

"So how do you explain the *HMS Highflyer* sinking that German cruiser not so far out in the Atlantic? And why do you think all but the neutral ships sail in convoys with cruiser escorts now?" challenged Reg.

"You sound like you want the war to be right here on Canadian soil," said Cassie accusingly.

"That's not going to happen." Jolene's voice was quick and firm.

"I expect you're right," replied Reg, "but with any luck, I'll be there in just three years."

"The war will be over by then," said Jolene.

"I hope not." Reg jumped off the boulder. "Not before me and my buddies Flynn and Edward get a chance to become flying aces like Billy Bishop and shoot down the Huns." He looked longingly at the sky, then at Michael. "Where will you enlist?"

Jolene had a momentary vision of Michael in a naval uniform. A shiver passed down her back. "Why would anyone enlist?" she asked. "The war will be over by this time next year."

Silence settled over the group. Reg regarded her suspiciously. Michael's expression was pensive. Cassie looked perplexed and anxious.

"Too many men have already died on the battlefield," Jolene stated boldly.

Reg's eyes narrowed.

"She has a point," admitted Michael. "I'm not sure I'd be in a hurry to enlist."

Reg spat on the ground. "A soldier ought to fear nothing but God and dishonour," he proclaimed before marching off to join his family.

"Don't mind Reg," said Cassie, falling into step beside

Michael. "There are others who feel like you do."

Michael smiled down at her. "Everyone is entitled to his own opinion. It's just a matter of maturity and perspective."

Jolene stumbled on a rock. Maturity and perspective? Those weren't words she typically associated with her brother. Besides, it was her opinion about the war that Michael had just echoed — an opinion that had taken shape inside her over the last few days and one, she realized, that she felt strongly about. A strand of Cassie's hair brushed her shoulder and she wondered if her friend shared her viewpoint.

Chapter Nine

Jolene hurried to catch up with Michael and Cassie who were still engaged in quiet conversation. The three of them made their way towards a small alcove on the edge of the woods. Grandpa was already there, speaking with a dark-haired man who could only be Cassie's father. A delicate woman with large sorrowful eyes sat on a bench in front of him. A toddler slept in her arms. Jolene noticed the black armband that she wore. A mother in mourning.

Missy ran towards Jolene as they approached. "Rory's telling a story," she whispered, pulling Jolene down onto the straw-like grass beside her while Cassie leaned against a tree trunk a few paces off to their right. Michael positioned himself next to Cassie, his arm extended behind her to reach the tree.

Jolene looked around at the faces assembled. There were probably two-dozen people and their attention was focused on a giant of a man with a bushy red moustache and beard. He seemed to be supporting a tree that had been bowed over by the wind.

A young woman, obviously pregnant, knelt on the edge of the circle. She had Cassie's dark hair and Missy's angelic, delicate features. She wore a wide, circular hat on her head and a sparkling emerald necklace around her neck. "Oh Rory, you're not intending to go on about Cape Breton again, are you?" she said, trying to look stern. "You make it sound like heaven."

Jolene wondered if Gerard considered it heavenly. She'd have to ask him.

"Ah, but Beth it is." The crowd groaned. "Cape Breton is a place where pockets of mist as white as fleece drift across the land. Where time is marked by the seasons, the rising of the sun and the length of the shadows on the shoreline. Where—"

"Angels descend with platters of succulent shrimp and red-backed lobster," mocked Beth.

Rory jumped into the centre of the circle and pulled his young wife to her feet.

"Ye shall see, my dear. This spring, once the bairn is born, I shall take ye both to Cape Breton."

"Assuming your shoulder is healed," replied Beth pragmatically.

Rory ignored her comment, but Jolene found herself wondering how much damage a bayonet could do. She watched Beth. At least her young husband had returned to her. How many terrifying nights had she lain awake fearing he wouldn't? And what would she have done if he hadn't?

"To Pleasant Bay we'll go, my love," Rory said, squeezing Beth's tiny hand so that it disappeared inside his enormous paw. "Ye shall soon call it heaven, Beth. I know ye will."

Beth shrugged her shoulders, but her eyes sparkled playfully. "It sounds like a pleasant place."

"More than pleasant." Rory released her hand. His eyes twinkled. "In the highlands, it is. Surrounded by trees and hills as far as the white-banded hawk can see. In the sunny haze of the sky, the hawk calls to the pilot whale swishing its tail in the salty spray. Waves lap gently at the beach and a road winds, following the curves of the shoreline, like those of a woman." He leaned close as if to kiss her, but, blushing, she pulled away.

"Serenaded by the flute-like song of the thrush, we shall stand high on the rocky cliffs and watch the blazing sunsets. Ye and the babe shall be lulled to sleep by the sound of the surf and awakened by the fury of her storms." He strode slowly about the circle. "But ye need not fear, my Beth. For the ocean is a woman who changes her complexion in the blink of an eye. A tempest who gives up her treasures as gifts from the sea." Rory reached for the emerald necklace at Beth's neck.

"He found it after a shipwreck," whispered Missy in Jo-lene's ear. "It was his wedding gift to her."

"Ye shall fall in love with Cape Breton, Beth, just as ye fell in love with me."

There was no doubt that Beth was as much in love with him as he was with her. Jolene pulled at a blade of grass an-ticipating the day when she too might feel that kind of love.

"You paint a heavenly picture, my dear," replied Beth, "but not once have you mentioned the snows of winter. How am I supposed to see those divine views when the snow on the trails is over my head?" She put one hand on her hip, bait-ing him.

Smiling, Rory skirted around behind her. Jolene, like the rest of the family, pressed forward. "Ah, but ye shall see those views even in the deepest of winters, my love. For I shall carry you atop my shoulders through the drifts."

The crowd chuckled.

Beth tossed her hair. "And what of the babe?" she chal-lenged playfully, laying a hand on her enlarged belly.

"The wee bairn will have the best view of all," replied Rory, his voice booming. "For he shall be seated atop your shoul-ders and you atop mine."

Missy broke into laughter. Rory surveyed Beth's family, his eyes lingering on Ma, whose lips had parted in a smile. "And when we have another, a lass with the angelic face of Missy," he said, brushing Missy's cheek with his rough fin-gers and causing the little girl's face to light up, "she shall ride high atop her brother's shoulders atop your shoulders atop my shoulders. And when our third child is born — "

"Oh stop!" cried Beth, trying to keep a straight face. "And how, Rory MacGregor, do you intend to provide for this ever-growing family of yours if you're constantly carrying us on your shoulders?" She crossed her arms across her chest in mock indignation.

"Nothing shall stop me!" proclaimed Rory. His voice thundered throughout the park. "I shall fish and hunt to feed my young. Hunt with my bare hands if I must. Grab the mighty stag by its antlers and bring it to its knees."

Beth giggled as Jolene and the others dissolved into laughter.

"And," said Rory, catching Ma's eye, "in the spring, when the young leaves have burst forth, when the first rose buds have unfurled, I shall find and capture a rare moose calf for my Beth to tame." The crowd roared. "Ye shall be the only woman in Cape Breton with a moose — a long-legged, gangly calf nuzzling yer shoulder, staring at ye with its big brown eyes." He stretched out his arms as if presenting his wife with this absurd gift.

Laughter burst from Beth. "Rory MacGregor, who's ever heard the likes of you?" she admonished. "You can no more tame a moose than you can tame a Scotsman." The crowd erupted and clapped as Rory swooped down on her and lifted her on his good shoulder. Watching them, Jolene felt an odd mixture of joy and envy. They were their own distinct selves and yet so completely together.

"Rory," cried Reg as the din died down and Beth was set

gently on her feet again. "Won't you tell us the story of the great Canadian victory at Vimy Ridge?"

A few others murmured in agreement, but Rory glanced towards Ma. A heavy sadness had returned to her eyes. The toddler in her arms fussed and Cassie's father reached for him. "Not today, Reg, my boy. But another time, I promise."

The listeners shifted and rose to their feet. People gathered coats and belongings. Jolene searched for Michael as Grandpa shook hands with Cassie's father and a few of the other men. Her brother still stood with his arm braced against the tree behind Cassie, who had turned to speak to him. He listened intently then laughed aloud. Jolene frowned. Michael's Ironman watch flashed in the waning light as Cassie swung around the trunk in Jolene's direction. Michael followed, a step behind her.

"Hey Cass, Pa said we can take the trails if we hurry!" Reg hustled towards them, his cap in his hands. "I bet I'll be the first to the Prince of Wales Tower."

"What are the trails?" asked Michael.

"Paths that lead through the park to the lookout tower and then out the other side to the tram station," replied Cassie. "It's farther than the walk along the beach, but we almost always beat the adults to the tram."

"We're super fast," explained Missy, grabbing Jolene's hand and pulling her towards the shaded trailhead. "Come on."

Reg raced for the path disappearing into the shadows

ahead of his little sister and Jolene, who glanced questioningly at Cassie and her brother. Michael hesitated, poised to
run.

"Go with Reg," urged Cassie. "You can catch him."

Michael took a few strides towards the trailhead and
stopped. "That's okay," he said, turning back towards them.
"I'll stay and escort you beautiful ladies."

Cassie giggled and Missy scrunched up her nose. "Your
brother's odd," she whispered to Jolene before starting towards the path.

"I heard that," said Michael, laughing. He stopped in the
sunlight. "We'd better tell Gramps where we're going, Jo.
You go ahead. I'll catch up." He crossed the grassy circle towards the bench where the adults were still mingling.

"I'll wait here so Michael doesn't get lost," offered Cassie.

Missy tugged at Jolene's hand then broke free, running
down the path that led through brush, clearings and over
grassy mounds. Jolene had no choice but to sprint after her,
Cassie's words echoing in her head. It was obvious that
Michael liked her new friend, but did she really like him or
was she just being kind? A branch snagged Jolene's hat and
she grabbed it from her hair, weaving left and right behind
Missy. They had reached a fork in the path, but the little girl
didn't hesitate. "This way," Missy insisted plunging down a
steep hill that seemed to disappear into a thicket of trees.

Jolene raced after her, glancing back periodically to see if
she could catch a glimpse of Cassie and Michael. Once she

thought she heard her brother's laugh, but the winding path made it difficult to see. A large tower loomed above them and Missy scrambled towards it. "Hurry," she called. "We're almost there."

They passed the Prince of Wales Tower and tore down a path that now seemed to straighten out before them. Jolene heard a distant clanging and emerged from the forested trail as the tram trundled into view.

"Good job!" called Grandpa, hustling towards them. "We only just arrived." He peered down the trail from which Jolene and Missy had just appeared. "Where's Michael?"

"He and Cassie should have left right behind us," said Jolene as the tram slowed on its approach to the station.

Missy scrunched up her nose. "They should be here by now."

Jolene took a few steps down the trail, listening for the telltale footsteps of people running. There was only silence. A throng of people gathered about the streetcar. "Should I go back?" she asked Grandpa.

"You'll miss the tram if you do," said Missy, moving in the direction of her parents. Jolene stood still, watching the concerned face of her grandfather.

"Hmm," pondered Grandpa stroking his moustache. A shriek pierced the air and Cassie and Michael came charging out of the trees.

"We made it!" Cassie exclaimed, catching sight of the tram and slowing her pace. Drops of perspiration beaded her forehead. She clutched her hat in one hand and waved it in the air. Panting, she and Michael joined Jolene and Grandpa.

"Halfway down the path I realized that my hat had fallen out of my coat pocket," Cassie explained, her breath coming in gulps. "We were both going to go back but we would never have made it. Michael sent me on and ran back for it."

"All the way to the start of the trailhead," added Michael, as the crowd surged forward towards the waiting tram. Rivers of sweat covered his temples and throat. "I caught up with her at the tower."

"Oh Jolene, I wish you'd been there. It was so crazy!" Cassie gripped Jolene's arm, her eyes wide and alive. "We thought we'd never make it but Michael can run so fast."

They had reached the doors of the tram. "Here, let me help you up," said Michael, offering Cassie a hand onto the streetcar.

"Thank you, you fleet-footed rescuer," said Cassie as Michael climbed up behind her.

Missy had saved Jolene a place near the front of the crowded tram. From her seat, she could not see Cassie and Michael standing behind her, but she could hear their voices and the occasional giggle. She resisted the temptation to turn around and watch them. It was exactly as she had told Grandpa it would be. Michael's bubbly nature and energy had overshadowed her again. It wasn't fair. Missy snuggled in against Jolene and soon drifted off into an angelic slumber.

"Michael seems to have fit right in," observed Grandpa from across the aisle.

Jolene scowled. "I knew this would happen. He comes with us for the first time and he's already stolen my friend." She glared over her shoulder where Michael's and Cassie's heads were bowed together.

"Or, perhaps," said Grandpa, watching them, "your friend has stolen Michael."

Chapter Ten

"You told me to be mature," protested Michael. He unfolded his towel and laid it on a sandy patch of shade beside the drinks cooler and beach chairs.

"Mature doesn't mean lavishing attention on every pretty girl you set eyes on." Jolene picked up the sunscreen and kicked off her flip-flops.

Michael looked up at the sky. "She is pretty, isn't she?" he said, almost to himself. He ignored Jolene's annoyed look and pulled his t-shirt off. "Anyway, I was just doing what you asked."

"Right!" How dare Michael twist this to make it seem like her doing. "'It's a pleasure to meet you, Cassie'," she mimicked. "'Let me help you up', and my all-time favourite, 'It's just a matter of maturity and perspective.'" Jolene rolled her eyes. "Three days ago, you were in hysterics watching choco-late milk spew out of a nine-year-old's nose and now it's Mr. Maturity himself?" A large dollop of sunscreen dripped into her palm. She slapped it on the back of her arms.

"It must be contagious."

"What?"

"Whatever you have that makes you change from one min-ute to the next. It must be contagious." Michael chuckled but his sister did not share his amusement. "At least I didn't embarrass you."

"Embarrass me? Of course you did."

"How?"

"Leaping over a raging fire on some stupid dare."

Michael grinned. "Hey, I had more sense than Reg."

"And racing through the trails like some cross-country star."

"I went back to get Cassie's hat."

"So you could show off!" The creamy liquid oozed between Jolene's fingers. "So Cassie and the whole world would know that 'Michael can run so fast.'"

"That's not true!" protested Michael. "And I am pretty fast; I'm in good shape." His green eyes darkened.

"It sounds like there's a storm brewing. Anything I can do?" Grandpa had come up behind them, his book bag in hand. He stood looking up at the sky, drenched in sun-shine, only a few wispy clouds in sight.

Jolene's gaze returned to Michael. "I didn't see you racing after Reg." She slapped the remainder of the sunscreen onto her arms and rubbed it in. "Cassie's my friend. She was just being kind to you because you're my twin brother."

Michael scooped up a handful of sand and let it fall between his fingers. "Do you think so?" he asked, genuinely concerned. "She didn't seem to mind my being around."

"Yeah, well she wants to be an actress," Jolene said spitefully.

"I know," said Michael. "She told me."

"She did, did she?" Cassie's revelation irked Jolene. She rubbed sunscreen violently onto her stomach. "And what other secrets has your girlfriend shared with you?"

"None, and what's it to you anyway?" Michael's voice rose. "And she's not my girlfriend!"

Grandpa unfolded a chair and collapsed into it. "Imagine," he said, grinning beneath his moustache, "having a girlfriend who was born a century ago."

Michael laughed. "That would be cool."

"See! You do like her." Jolene squirted a long stream of white cream onto her left leg. Grandpa leaned back in his chair.

"So what if I do like her? I'm almost thirteen," Michael said, echoing Jolene's words on the plane. He kicked at the sand with his bare foot, sending a shower of brown grit across Jolene's sticky leg.

"Look what you've done!" She tried to brush the sand off her shin, but only succeeded in covering her hands in a dirty, slimy mess. She stomped off in the direction of the ocean.

Having rinsed the sand off her leg, she looked back over her shoulder at Michael. She should never have taken him through the time crease. She waded into the water, gasping as the cool waves lapped at her belly. She should never have trusted him with their secret. The water was colder than she'd imagined, but she dove in anyway, hoping the salty waves would wash away her frustration. Floating on her back, she stole a glance up the beach. Grandpa was reading his fat history book. Michael, too, had obviously pulled a book out of Grandpa's book bag and was reading it.

Jolene made her way back to the water's edge. She'd only applied sunscreen to one leg, but she didn't care if she burnt the other one. She meandered up the beach, looking for shells and shiny bits of sea glass. What, she wondered, was Gerard doing right now?

"Stay there!" Dad called. He and Mom were strolling down the beach towards her. Jolene stopped and forced a smile to her lips as Dad raised the camera and took a picture. "Okay, now how about one with you and Mom?"

Jolene stayed where she was and her mother joined her. "I thought you and Michael would be out beachcombing or swimming." She posed for the photo, one arm draped around Jolene's shoulders.

"I don't feel like it right now."

"Say lobsters," ordered Dad.

Jolene tilted her head towards her mother and curled the edges of her lips upwards. She heard the camera click and let her body droop.

"I'm going to go inland to get some long shots," called Dad from beneath his floppy hat.

Mom waved at him, then let her hand slide down Jolene's arm. "Why so glum?"

Jolene shrugged. "I wish I wasn't a twin." Catching the surprised look on her mother's face, she continued quickly. "It's just so hard to have your own friends and be your own person when there's always two of you." She watched the surf breaking on the rocks.

"For years, you wanted to be identical twins," Mom replied, smiling. "Even though you've always been so different." She tousled Jolene's hair. "Friends are important, but they can never replace family. Often when friends can or will no longer help, family can and will."

Jolene mulled over her mother's remark. She had heard it from her parents many times and seen it first-hand when they had taken her grandfather in. "Because family members have to be responsible for each other?"

"Yes," agreed Mom, "but it's more than that. When you really know someone with all their faults and still love them, you love them in a very special way."

"So family ties really are unbreakable," said Jolene, quoting the message on the slate.

"In some ways, I suppose." For a moment the two of them

stood watching the surf. "But that doesn't mean you have to spend all your time with Michael. At your age, it's only natural to want some independence." A wave lapped at their feet. "Does Michael feel that way, too?"

"I don't think so or at least he doesn't seem to."

"Well, if he doesn't need his independence now, he will soon. Girls mature faster than boys, that's all."

Cassie's mother had told Cassie the same thing.

"I know it's hard on holidays because you're together more often," said Mom, "but try and be patient. This trip won't last forever and you two have always had a special bond." She gestured towards the patch of shade that Michael and Grandpa occupied. "I need a cold drink. Want to walk back with me?"

Jolene buried her toes in the wet sand. "No thanks. I think I'll wander up to the point."

"Okay," said Mom, her words almost drowned out by the squawking of the seagulls overhead.

Jolene watched the birds dip and glide on the wind above their ocean playground. A tiny red crab scuttled sideways and disappeared down a hole. Her mother was right. She didn't have to spend all her time with Michael, especially not in 1917 where safety wasn't such a big concern. Jolene wandered past two broken lobster traps and through stringy sections of green nets that littered the beach. She and Cassie had hit it off right away. They'd had a wonderful first day together and they would have had a great time at Point Pleasant Park, too, if it hadn't been for Michael. Jolene leaped over a log and began to run through the waves, leaving a path of temporary footsteps behind her. The next time they went back to 1917, she'd just tell Michael that she wanted some time on her own with Cassie. There was something invigorating about that thought and she ran faster. At the rocky point, the wind gusted. She took a deep breath of the salty mist, wishing that she could fly.

Something sparkled in the waves and Jolene reached down as the tide came in. Her hand closed around a metal object — a rusted brooch. She rinsed it in the water, noticing that it was shaped like a bird. Its eye, probably a shiny stone, was missing. Setting it on a piece of driftwood in the sun, she waded out into the waves.

"What treasures has the sea decided to give up today?"

Jolene turned at the sound of her grandfather's voice. "Hey Gramps! I found an old brooch, but that's about it."

"You never know what you might find on the beach."

"Rory found Beth's emerald necklace after a shipwreck."

Grandpa stared out at the water glistening in the sun. "It's hard to imagine that this same ocean can turn into a dangerous tempest, isn't it?" He settled himself on one end of the driftwood and Jolene joined him.

"Were there lots of shipwrecks on the shores of Nova Scotia?"

"Halifax is a big port. Many ships left from and sailed for this port over the years. Not all of them arrived safely at their destinations."

"Because of storms?"

"Storms, pirates, icebergs, the mistakes of men." Jolene and Grandpa turned at the sound of a gruff voice behind them. An elderly man with skin the colour of milk chocolate stood on the rocks. A toothpick hung from the corner of his mouth and a coarse grey stubble covered his cheeks and chin. He shuffled past Jolene and took a seat on the driftwood log, nodding at Grandpa.

"I imagine there's more than one tale of the sea that'd fill a sunny afternoon," said Grandpa invitingly. Jolene grinned at her grandfather. He never missed a chance to hear or tell a story.

The man chewed on his toothpick. "Good thing for us sailors that wood floats," he said pointing at a bulky piece of wood bobbing up and down close to shore.

Jolene cast a puzzled look at her grandfather who leaned forward into the tale.

"Floating wood. It was what she was carrying when the crew set sail just days before Christmas. Lumber. Cut and stacked in the hold. To be delivered to the Barbados. A pleasant run or so they thought on the little brigantine . . ." He paused. "What did you say your name was?" he asked Jolene.

"Jolene," she answered shyly.

"A pleasant run or so they thought on the little brigantine *Jolene.*"

Jolene grinned. She followed the sailor's gaze towards the water almost expecting to see the square sail of an old brigantine ship billowing in the wind.

"They weren't far out when the first blast of a North Atlantic storm hit them. It was a bad one." He removed the toothpick from his mouth. "A monster gale in heavy seas. All day she hammered the *Jolene,* raging like an angry daughter of Neptune, until the ship let go and sprang a leak. The crew cut the rigging, fighting to stay upright. But when the foremast broke away and the main topmast went ... well, they stopped fighting and started surviving." The old sailor cleared his throat. "They climbed onto the roof of the forehouse, clung on with frozen fingers and waited for the daylight."

"There's hope in the dawn," agreed Grandpa.

"So they thought, but the daylight arrived with a nightmare in tow. Mountains of waves that smashed the stern of the *Jolene* and ripped her apart." The old sailor grunted. "And sent the lifeboats drifting out to sea."

"What did they do?" Jolene's voice was soft and small.

"What could they do? The ship was disintegrating beneath their feet. But she didn't sink." The old sailor grinned at Jolene, his grey eyes narrow slits in his weathered face. "Full of wood, she was and wood floats." He pointed triumphantly at the wood bobbing lazily off shore. "Nevertheless," he added, "it weren't exactly an ideal situation."

"I should hardly think so." Grandpa caught the sailor's eye and the two men laughed.

"By Christmas Eve, the men were missing the candles on the trees back home, so they decided they'd soak a few jackets in oil and light them on fire. See if any other vessel on

the seas might want to join in their Christmas festivities."
He sighed. "But they had no takers." He paused to examine
his toothpick. "Then they figured that they ought to think
about Christmas dinner. The ship was still afloat and the
galley stove was housed in the forehouse. There was no reason they couldn't rustle up a little something on such a special occasion. It's amazing what you can concoct with
bread, rum and turnips." The sailor repositioned his toothpick between two back teeth and winked at Jolene.

"Food is overrated, but water is not." He gestured out to
sea. "So much and so salty." He leaned towards Jolene, his
shoulder brushing hers. "Do you know what they did?"

She shook her head.

"Now think about it before you go shaking your head.
You must have learned something in school." He straightened up, his back creaking. "Remember, they had themselves a stove and more salt water than a blue whale could
want."

Jolene tilted her chin towards the grey eyes and then
glanced back at Grandpa who was stroking his moustache
in thought. Her mind raced. She and Michael had done an
experiment earlier in the year. A bowl of salt water in a
sealed plastic bag set in the sunshine. The water had evap-
orated and condensed on the sides of the bag. When she and
Michael had tasted the condensed water droplets, they'd discovered fresh water. "They boiled the sea water," she began
cautiously, "and then condensed the steam from it to make
fresh water."

The sailor slapped his palms against his pant legs. "You'd be a good one to have along on a shipwreck." He winked at Jolene again and smiled approvingly at her grandfather.

"She's an ideas person, all right," replied Grandpa.

Jolene smiled proudly. "Did it work?"

"Every man was allowed a few tablespoons of water each day. Enough to keep them alive to fight the next winter gale that arrived."

"No!" Grandpa's face reflected Jolene's sense of unfairness.

"Yes, but this was a lucky storm."

"There's such a thing as a lucky storm?" asked Jolene.

"There is when it blows a big liner off course in your direction." The chocolate-skinned man's chuckle squeezed out around his toothpick. "A big ocean liner, thrown off course, but too late for Christmas."

"But not too late?" said Grandpa.

"No, although none too early. No sooner had the crew climbed aboard the liner than the *Jolene* was bashed to pieces. Saved by a fluke of fate they were."

Jolene stared out at the sea, marvelling at fate and how it shaped lives in an uncontrollable way.

"Every time I see a piece of wood wash up on shore, I can't help wondering if it isn't that very same cargo that kept those sailors alive through Christmas." The old man pushed himself to his feet. "Good thing wood floats," he said, winking at Jolene and shaking Grandpa's hand.

"A very good thing or we might not have been treated to

such an entertaining tale," replied Grandpa, gripping the man's brown hand with both of his.

The old sailor raised his arm in a gesture of farewell and made his way around the rocky point. Jolene stood beside Grandpa and watched him shuffle away. "So much of life is determined by fate."

Grandpa put an arm around her shoulders and steered her in the direction of their beach chairs. "Yes," he said, "and no. Your decisions have a lot to do with how your life unfolds, Jo." He fiddled with his moustache. "But sometimes there are things that you can't control. Then you just have to hope that fate is kind."

Jolene dug her toes into the sand, wondering if fate would be kind to her.

"Jolene, Dad, over here." Her dad was waving at them from beneath the blue and white striped awning of the concession stand. "I need a few extra hands." He held up two dripping ice-cream cones.

"Looks like fate's being kind right now," said Jolene as she ran to help her father.

Trickles of sticky blueberry ice cream ran down Jolene's fingers by the time they reached Mom and Michael. Jolene handed her mother a strawberry cone and settled into the shade.

"What are you reading, Michael?" asked Dad.

"Gramps lent me a book about World War One. It's pretty interesting stuff, especially now that — "

"We're in Halifax where the explosion took place," interrupted Jolene. She gave Michael a warning glance. He licked his ice cream.

"It's going to be a good exhibit," said Dad confidently. He turned towards his father. "I hope you're finding some good stories."

"Don't worry about that," said Jolene, smiling smugly but offering no explanation.

"Gramps always finds good stories," said Michael. "Like that one about Cape Breton that we heard at . . ." Grandpa coughed and Michael's voice trailed off when he realized his error. "I forget where we were," he muttered.

A seagull screeched overhead and Dad rose to his feet. "I think I'll go for a quick dip before it's time to go. Anybody coming?"

"Sure," said Mom, joining Dad in the sunshine.

"I will as soon as I'm done my cone," Michael told them.

"I think I'll stay in the shade for a bit," said Jolene, pressing two fingers on her burnt right leg and leaving two temporary white lines. Her parents headed for the water's edge.

"Boy, you really have to watch what you say in the present and the past," Michael said after their parents were out of hearing distance. He grinned at his sister. "Don't be scared to interrupt me for my own good."

Jolene pointed at Michael's Ironman watch. "In that case, next time we go back, take your watch off. That'd be pretty hard to explain in 1917." She finished her ice cream and stretched out on her towel as Michael joined her parents in the water and Grandpa resumed reading.

Her thoughts drifted from Michael to the old sailor to Cassie. What did fate have in store for Cassie and her family, Rory and Beth? They were all living in Richmond, the area of Halifax that had been destroyed by the explosion. Almost two thousand people had died and another nine thousand had been injured. Again, she heard Rory's deep belly laugh, felt Cassie's embrace and saw Missy snuggle in beside her on the tram. She couldn't, she knew, change history. On the morning of the explosion, those warm, caring people would be struck by a disaster bigger than anything they could imagine. Would fate be kind to them?

Chapter Eleven

"Cassie and Reg won't even be home," protested Jolene the next afternoon. She and Michael had just said goodbye to Grandpa at the North Street Railway Station and arranged to meet back there at three o'clock. "They'll be at school."

"Oh well, I just want to know where they live. What's wrong with that?" Michael was three steps in front of Jolene, urging her along.

Jolene sighed. At least exploring the town was better than hanging around the railway station. She'd show him Cassie's house and then go down to the dock. With any luck, Michael would find something interesting at the wharf and she could leave him there and meet Cassie when Richmond School let out. "All right," she agreed, striding along Campbell Road.

The tram rolled by them, stopping traffic and exciting a horse pulling a milk wagon. Two uniformed soldiers passed, deep in conversation. A ship's whistle sounded in the distance and a car horn blared.

"I like 1917," Michael said, his cheeks dimpling. "It's full of life."

"And death," murmured Jolene as more uniformed men passed them.

"Yeah, I stayed up late reading that book on the war. It was pretty awful. Now I know why you weren't keen on enlistment."

"It's not just about being scared to die," explained Jolene. "It's the whole idea of Canada going to war to defend Britain even though Canada is no longer a colony. Was it really her war?"

Michael shrugged. "The Americans didn't join in until 1918, until it was almost over."

"Turn left," instructed Jolene as they reached the intersection of Roome Street and Campbell Road. They headed uphill, Mulgrave Park on their left.

Michael pointed at a large rambling house on the corner, badly in need of paint. A wooden sign had been nailed to the front door. "Why is there a *Quarantine* sign on that house?"

"They probably have some contagious illness," said Jolene, remembering Cassie's story of scarlet fever. She stopped in front of Cassie's home. "This is their place."

Michael stood, his feet firmly planted in the dirt road. A

shape distorted the shadow of a tree and Cat emerged from the darkness, purring loudly. She rubbed herself against Jolene's legs in greeting.

"Hello Cat," said Jolene stroking her back. "Will you show us your kittens today?" She turned towards Michael, suddenly remembering Missy's offer and wondering if she could ever convince her brother to change his mind. "They're under the shed behind the house." They followed Cat around to the back of the building.

"Oh no!" Cassie's voice, on the verge of tears, came from behind a half-secured sheet on a clothesline. The wind had whipped a corner of the sheet free of its peg and it now trailed in the dirt. Cassie stepped out from behind a fluttering skirt and rescued it from the ground.

"Hello," called Jolene.

Cassie looked up, her hair blowing wildly about. Streaks of white powder covered her cheeks and forehead and a soiled apron hid the front of her dress.

"Jolene." Cassie's voice was surprised but excited. "Michael," she added, with a smile. The sound of glass shattering came from the house. "Ben!" she screamed before disappearing inside. A child howled. The dirty unpegged corner of the sheet drifted back towards the dirt. Jolene and Michael darted simultaneously for the back door and arrived as Cassie emerged, holding Ben, his finger bleeding. "Shh! Shh!" she said trying to comfort her little brother whom Jolene recognized from Point Pleasant Park.

"Here." Michael pulled a handkerchief from his pocket

and wound the soft cotton around the little boy's finger before tying it in a knot. A few spots of red seeped through the cloth, but the child stopped crying.

"Oh thank you," said Cassie. "It's been such a busy morning and . . ." She stopped. "But I'm forgetting my manners. Won't you come in?" She wiped a white streak from her damp forehead and held the back door open.

The smell of yeast mingled with a strong, clean scent coming from a pot boiling on the coal stove. A shirtsleeve dangled from its edge. Cassie set Ben safely down in a crib on one side of the room and pushed a plate that might have been within his reach out of harm's way. She snatched up a whiskbroom and dustpan and swept up the remains of a broken mug.

"We thought you'd be at school," said Jolene.

"But we're glad you're not," added Michael quickly.

Cassie sighed. "I should be, but Ma's not well today." She tugged at the bottom of her apron. "On bad days, she goes to the cemetery and just sits there. I don't know why. James' body isn't there, but . . ." Her voice trailed off and despair filled the room. Jolene moved towards her friend who seemed so vulnerable.

Cassie's chin jerked up. "Since I had to stay home and look after Ben, I thought I'd do the wash and a few chores," she said, suddenly sounding very adult-like. She gestured helplessly around the kitchen, which was still cluttered with dirty breakfast dishes. A dusting of flour covered the table and the pot on the stove boiled over, hissing on the hot surface. "Unfortunately, it's not as easy as it looks when Ma does it." Laughing, Cassie held up a charcoal piece of toast on a pronged fork.

Jolene felt a pang of sympathy for her friend. The war had made it necessary for Cassie, barely a teenager, to take on an adult's role and all its responsibilities. Caught between the two roles, she seemed to switch from one to the other without warning.

"Please," she said jumping back into the adult role, "I just have a few things to finish up and then I'll make us some tea." She strode towards an adjoining door. "Why don't you wait in here."

They followed her into a dimly lit room furnished with a sofa and two old armchairs. These were strewn with afghans and half-finished knitting. A stack of newspapers had slid off the coffee table onto the floor. "I'll be right back," said Cassie, disappearing into the kitchen.

Jolene and Michael wandered around the room. An unshaded lamp sat on an end table and illuminated a framed photo of a young man in uniform.

Jolene reached out and picked up the picture of the laughing young soldier. A telegram, its edges worn, also lay on the table. Michael bent his head to read it aloud. "Deeply regret to inform you, Private James Caldwell, infantry, officially reported killed in action . . ." Michael's voice died and they read the remaining words in silence.

"I wonder how he died," whispered Jolene, glancing at the door to the kitchen.

Michael pointed at a stack of articles carefully clipped from the newspaper. *Passchendaele Won at Terrible Cost* exclaimed one headline. *Hand to Hand Fighting by our Troops* read another. "It was a slaughter in the mud," said Michael. "I read about it in the book Gramps lent me."

Jolene looked down at the joyful eyes of the soldier in the photo.

"That's my brother James." Jolene set the picture down and turned towards Cassie's voice in the doorway. She had removed her apron and pinned her hair up in a bun. She looked, thought Jolene, like the elegant lady of the house.

Cassie rocked onto her toes and back down onto her heels. "He was killed almost a month ago at Passchendaele."

"I'm sorry," murmured Michael. They stood staring at the floor.

"I put the kettle on for tea," said Cassie finally. "I'll . . ." Her words were drowned out by the bawling of Ben. "Oh no, I forgot his milk." The toddler shrieked again and Cassie sank onto the sofa, a child again. "I try," she said absently, "but it's so hard and I don't know what I'll do if Ma doesn't get better soon."

Her despair tugged at Jolene's heart. She crossed the room, perched on the arm of the sofa and put one arm around Cassie's shoulder.

Ben let out another cry and Cassie sank farther into the

sofa, away from Jolene's embrace. "It's been almost a month now and it just gets worse and worse. I don't think she's ever coming back. And with Beth gone, all the household chores fall to me. I can't handle it."

"There's so much to do," said Michael sympathetically. He sat down on the sofa beside Cassie. "It's an impossible situation." In the kitchen, Ben's shrieks turned to whimpers.

Jolene stared at the gloomy, resigned faces of Cassie and her brother and felt an unexpected surge of determination within her. "No it's not!" she said leaping to her feet. Both Cassie and Michael looked up. "You have a big, close family, lots of aunts and uncles and cousins and you know all your neighbours. You don't have to do this alone, Cassie." Cassie had raised her chin and was watching Jolene with dull blue eyes. "There's no shame in asking for help when you need it."

A faint light illuminated Cassie's eyes. Slowly, she rose to her feet.

"Reg can help with the chores," said Jolene.

"He never does women's work."

"But he could." Jolene pointed at Michael. "Michael helps with dishes some days."

"Really?"

Michael nodded, but his eyes looked puzzled.

"These are unusual circumstances and unusual times." Jolene joined Cassie in the centre of the messy room. "What harm would there be in asking for help?"

Cassie shrugged. "None, I guess."

Jolene clasped her friend's hands. "It wouldn't have to be much. Why I bet that if we put our minds and hands to it, we could have this place cleaned up in no time."

Cassie's lips parted in a smile. "I bet we could, too."

"So let's do it."

"Oh Jolene!" Cassie caught her hand. "You'd do that for me?"

"Why not?" asked Jolene. "Wouldn't you do the same for me?"

"Absolutely!" replied Cassie. She stood upright, looking proud and defiant and then, suddenly, sheepish. "I can't believe I ever thought about giving up."

"Giving up?" The front door slammed and Beth breezed into the room. "Those words from a sister of mine, no less."

"Beth!" Cassie ran towards the door. "Jolene and I were just about to start tidying up." Her sister deposited her coat and hat on the back of an armchair and bustled into the kitchen. She re-emerged with Ben in her arms, his chubby legs straddling her round belly. "I thought you were volunteering at the hospital today," said Cassie.

"I was," replied Beth. "But I ran into Mrs. Dorchester and she told me she'd seen Ma at the cemetery, so I stopped at Elizabeth Bell's place and told her to tell them I'd be in on Thursday morning instead."

"Oh Beth!" Cassie hugged her sister. "I'm so glad you're here."

Beth gestured towards the kitchen. "I can see that," she said, grinning. "I'll tell you what. I'll set things right here, if you'll do me a favour." She handed Cassie a few coins. "Stop by the store and pick up some sage for that roast that's been set out for dinner and then run down to the shipping warehouse and tell Rory to join me here for supper." Ben fussed and Beth hushed him. "Now, off you all go so you're not underfoot." She glanced at a clock on an end table. "I don't suppose there's any point going to school today," she said winking at Cassie, then at Jolene and Michael.

"Oh thank you, Beth, thank you." Cassie's eyes had regained their usual sparkle. "Whatever shall I do without you when you're gone to Cape Breton?"

"Never mind that," said Beth. "Now away with you."

Chapter Twelve

Cassie skipped down Campbell Road in front of Michael and Jolene, money jingling in the pocket of her coat. "Let's go to the shipping yards first," she suggested. "I'll pick up the sage on the way home."

"Okay," agreed Jolene, still hoping that Michael might find something to amuse himself with at the wharf so that she and Cassie could spend time alone.

The railyards were busy and noisy and so too were the piers they passed. Sailors milled around the docks and soldiers seemed to materialize and disappear into the crowds. "Hey, isn't that your brother?" asked Jolene, pointing towards a group of boys with bicycles. They were clustered around a sailor who was leaning against a lamppost, a cigarette in his hand. Smoke curled lazily above their heads.

"It better not be," said Cassie. She marched towards the boys, stopping just behind them. "Reg!" Reg jumped at the sound of his name. He wheeled his bicycle towards his sister, two boys his age trailing behind him. "Father will be furious if he finds out that you've been truant!"

"Yeah, well, he doesn't have to find out, does he?" Reg stared defiantly at her. "We've been looking for spies," he told them. "Me and Flynn and Edward." He gestured from one boy to the other.

Flynn, a red-headed boy with large ears protruding from beneath his cap, looked suspiciously at both Michael and Jolene. He leaned towards Edward and whispered in the dark-eyed boy's ear.

"All of you are in big trouble!" fumed Cassie, making Jolene wonder if all sisters had issues with their brothers. "You and your spies."

Cassie turned away and continued along Campbell Road. Michael and Jolene followed, glancing back over their shoulders at the boys who had returned to the sailor's stories. They passed a rambling wood-frame building with a group of children playing tag in the yard. "That's the Protestant Orphanage," Cassie told them. Jolene smiled. Before they left Halifax, the clothes that she and Michael were now wearing would be left for those children.

"And just a few blocks farther on are the Wellington Barracks and the Admiralty House," said Cassie, continuing her guided tour. "They have magazines full of ammunition there in case the Germans attack." A short while later, they crossed the street and soon their boots were clip-clopping across the wooden wharves towards a large fifteen-storey building that dominated the landscape. "This is the Acadia Sugar Refinery. Raw bales of sugar cane are shipped here and made into sugar."

"What a stench!" retorted Michael as a sweet, burning smell assaulted their noses.

"And over here, at this pier, is where Rory works." They had walked behind the sugar refinery and now found themselves in a large shipping yard. Horses transporting goods tossed their heads. Harnesses and bits rattled. Men called back and forth. Cassie led the way to a large warehouse. "Rory is a security guard. Look, there he is now." She raced towards a man standing near the door of the warehouse. Jolene and Michael arrived on her heels as Reg, Flynn and Edward rode up behind them.

"What's all this?" asked Rory, regarding them curiously. "Has school been cancelled on account of a lack of students?" He stroked his beard.

Cassie cleared her throat. "I stayed home because of Ma," she explained. "But you'll have to ask Reg and his buddies why they've declared today a holiday." Her pretty face challenged her brother.

Reg shuffled his feet. "We were looking for spies," he whispered. "Out at Point Pleasant Park."

Rory let out a barking laugh. "Spies? Ye don't say. Right here in Halifax?"

"There's some Germans here," declared Flynn. "Germans who claim to be Canadians, but who could be signalling German submarines from the point, you know."

Rory's amused expression changed to a sober one. "Now just because a man's got a German-sounding name, that don't mean he's a spy, son." He squinted at Flynn. "Don't be too quick to go making unfounded claims, ye hear me. Ye'll do more harm than good." He reached into his coat pocket. "I been over there, on the front, fighting against them German boys and I reckon they feel those bayonets just like we do." He rubbed his shoulder.

Jolene noticed the puzzled expression on Flynn's face. She was just as confused. One of those German soldiers had sliced Rory's shoulder with a bayonet, and yet here he was almost defending the enemy.

"Will you tell us the story of Vimy Ridge?" asked Reg. "You promised."

"That I did. And I don't suppose there's any time like the present." Rory pulled a stick of chewing gum out of his pocket and folded it into his mouth before beginning.

Jolene watched his face, wondering what picture he would paint of the war.

"I still remember the first time I laid eyes on Vimy Ridge — a ridge with a high crest known as Hill 145 and, on its northern end, a knoll called the Pimple." Edward snickered. "Vimy Ridge — bristling with machine guns and guarded by German trenches and dugouts."

Rory chewed thoughtfully. "We were training in England

when the order came for the 85th Nova Scotia Highlanders to move out to the front. We was itchin' to go, to do battle with the rest of the 4th Division. Except it weren't for fighting we went, but for support. That meant digging trenches and building roads. It weren't glamorous work, but at least we were at the front, close to the action, and we put our backs into it." Rory stood tall.

"For months, our lads had been preparing for the attack on Vimy. Some had laid railway tracks to transport ammunition, troops and food. Some had constructed plank roads through the mud to move equipment. And," he paused to stress the importance of his next words, "some of the lads had dug a series of tunnels all the way from our trenches, through no-man's land and — unknown to the Germans — deep under enemy lines." Edward gasped. All eyes were riveted on Rory. "Tunnels big enough to house a light railway, water and electrical lines. There were even communication cables so that the lads didn't lose contact with headquarters."

"Didn't they use pigeons and flares to communicate, too?" asked Michael.

"Aye, they did," acknowledged Rory.

Reg stared hard at Michael as Rory continued. "Every day, the boys rehearsed their roles, using their scale models of the German position. There weren't a man among them who didn't know to the wee details exactly what he had to do to win Vimy Ridge."

He wagged a thick finger at them. "The success of the

attack depended on the success of all four divisions. If every division did its job, by the end of the day, Vimy Ridge would belong to the Allies."

"On Easter Monday," added Michael. Jolene looked up, surprised. He must have spent all night reading up on World War One.

"Right ye are," said Rory, impressed. "The preparatory bombardment had been going on for two weeks and by the day of the attack, the Germans were hurting. But little did they know that by the end of that day, they'd be hurting even more."

The children edged in closer to Rory, forming a tight circle around him. Cassie's hand squeezed Jolene's.

"At five in the morning of April 9th, the nightly bombardment died down and silence fell — a silence as thick as a blanket of fog. It was almost peaceful, it was. But half an hour later, in blowing sleet, the battle began. The artillery lit up the sky and the roar of shells mixed with the rattling of machine-gun fire. The infantry soldiers climbed out of their trenches and followed the artillery units. We stood and watched the lads move into the shell-torn no-man's land with rifles and bayonets in hand."

Jolene shuddered as Rory paused. Now would come the tales of horror she had already heard too often.

"We stayed in the trenches listening to the sounds of the battle, hearing the reports come in. The German front-line fell quickly to the 1st Division and they pressed on towards the second trench line. There were casualties, but by dusk, the German prisoners were pouring towards the Allied lines."

Flynn rubbed his palms together.

"The 2nd Division attacked with the swiftness of an eagle. Why, in one dugout behind enemy lines, they even found a bunch of German officers enjoying a fancy lunch served by waiters in uniforms." The boys mimed the scene, making everyone laugh.

"The Germans were so certain that Vimy Ridge couldn't be taken," said Michael as the laughter subsided. Jolene was beginning to suspect that she had been wrong about this story ending in tragedy and horror.

"But ye know what, lad," said Rory. "They were wrong." His eyes gleamed. "The 3rd Division's attack went like clock-work and by late in the afternoon, they were in control of key positions on Hill 145. Everything was going according to plan . . . except for the 4th Division." He lowered his voice. "The artillery bombardment hadn't destroyed the German front-line trenches in front of Hill 145. As soon as the shelling stopped, the Germans poured out of the ditch-es and rained machine-gun fire on our lads, caught out in the open. The Huns had the high ground, you see, and our boys were in trouble. All might have been lost right there if a brave Canadian Scot hadn't snaked through the trenches and destroyed two machine gun posts that were slaughter-ing our boys. The 4th started to move forward again, but they were in a bad way. They'd suffered huge losses and darkness was falling."

Jolene's head ached. Maybe she'd been right about the bad ending after all.

Rory tensed his broad shoulders. "That's when the orders came for the 85th to take up their arms and capture Hill 145." The brightness of his eyes mesmerized Jolene. "We hadn't had any real battle experience, but we had spirit and determination. We raced through our trenches until we could see the Germans standing on Hill 145, waiting for us to attack. Only they hadn't reckoned on us being Cape Bretoners." He chuckled. "We approached the hill at a run, screaming at the top of our lungs and charging at the enemy. They fired at us and explosions shook the ground. Bullets whizzed past us but we just kept on coming. I stumbled into a dugout with two German soldiers and struck the first one down with my bayonet. His comrade lunged for my heart, but I jerked away and the blade severed my shoulder. I plunged my own bayonet into him and left him slumped in the mud."

Rory inclined his head towards them. Jolene searched for the haunted look she'd seen on Andrew's face, but could see only passion and pride. "We must have been quite a sight, because most of the remaining Germans turned tail and ran." He looked around at the eyes riveted on his face. "Vimy Ridge was ours!"

"Victory!" Edward screamed, pumping his fist in the air.

"Aye," agreed Rory. "And from the top of Vimy Ridge, we could see the valley on the other side — lush, green, unmarked by the shells and horror of war."

"I wish I could have been there," said Reg passionately, "for Canada."

Rory nodded. "The Canadians saved the day and the other troops respected our audacity and courage."

"They should have given you a medal," said Flynn, "for bravery."

Rory smiled. "Every one of those lads out there deserved a medal," he said. "For bravery! For courage! For freedom!"

Jolene watched Reg and his friends celebrate the glory of victory. Rory and so many others like him had fought and killed in the belief that it was their duty and right to do so. And James and so many others like him had fought and been killed in that same belief. Jolene's head throbbed.

Michael had stepped back from the circle and stood beside his sister. "Victory at a heavy price," he said slowly. The other boys glared at him.

"It was a dear one," admitted Rory, "but necessary." He stretched. "I had better be getting back to my patrolling and ye had better be running off to do yer errands. What might they be anyway?"

"Oh," said Cassie, smiling at him. "Beth sent me to tell you to join her at our place for supper. She's cooking a roast."

"Where there's food is where I'll be," promised Rory. He frowned at the boys. "And I don't expect yer spy-watching activities will be taking ye out of school again."

"No sir," replied Flynn. "I'll be needing that education if I'm going to join the Air Force." The boys pedalled away and Michael and Jolene bade Rory goodbye.

They followed Cassie back along the wharf, neither of them speaking. Cassie stopped to watch the action at Pier 6. The *S.S. Picton*, an enormous freighter, was waiting for repairs. A crew of men were unloading her cargo while the captain kept strict watch over them. "Reg says there's explosives on board the *Picton*," said Cassie, "but I don't believe him." Nearby, a couple of smaller, wooden tugs were moored.

The three children ambled onwards. Jolene turned at the sound of rubber tires squealing behind them. Reg, Edward and Flynn had arrived on their bicycles. "Hey you!" cried Flynn. He was staring at Michael.

Edward leaped off his bicycle and approached them. "Reg tells us you wouldn't be in a hurry to enlist," he said, eyeing Michael critically.

"So?" challenged Michael.

"So," muttered Reg. "I find it just a little odd that yesterday you didn't even know what a patrol boat was and today, well, you know an awful lot about Vimy Ridge."

"Who's giving you information?" snarled Edward, grabbing Michael's wrist before he could respond. "And who are you informing on?"

Michael tried to jerk his arm away. The sleeve of his jacket slid up his forearm to reveal his Ironman watch. It beeped twice indicating that it was two o'clock. Edward let go of his arm and jumped back. "He's got a bomb."

Jolene gasped, but before Michael could react, Flynn had grabbed the front of Michael's jacket and was staring threateningly at her brother. "Start talking, spy-boy. I seen all those dials and numbers on your watch. You're going tell us what they're for — or maybe you'd like to tell the authorities about this new German technology."

"Yeah," agreed Edward. "I bet our side would like to know what you know."

"You're crazy!" Michael gave a sudden push and sent Flynn stumbling to the ground. The red-haired boy got to his feet, his fists clenched, as Edward and Reg circled behind Michael.

"Stop it!" cried Jolene, positioning herself between Michael and Flynn. "He's not spying for the Germans." She glared at Michael. She'd already warned him about wearing his watch in the past. In some ways it would serve him right if he got beat up. But at the same time her brain was working frantically to find some explanation.

The boys continued to regard them skeptically. "Our mother gave me this watch," said Michael.

An idea was starting to take shape in Jolene's mind. She covered her mouth, her eyes wide with mock horror. "Michael!" she reprimanded him. "That's top secret information and you know it."

Michael stared at her as if she'd gone crazy.

Jolene glanced sideways at Reg and his friends. "We took an oath," she said, lowering her voice and winking at her brother.

A sudden look of understanding crossed Michael's face. He swallowed a smile. "I know. I forgot," he murmured apologetically.

The boys looked from Jolene to Michael and back to Jolene.

"When I first met her, Jolene told me that her mother had come here for meetings at the university," offered Cassie uncertainly.

Reg glanced at Flynn and Edward. Then his mouth fell open and his eyes bulged. "You, you mean, that your mother is here working for *our* side?"

Jolene scrutinized him then looked away, wondering where to go from here.

"You mean you have access to top-secret information about the war?" breathed Edward, his voice streaked with wonder.

Jolene looked questioningly at Michael. He shrugged.

"You can trust us," said Flynn, misinterpreting their exchange. "We're all cadets and we've been scouting out German submarines for the past three years."

Jolene could sense their eagerness. She tried not to let her amusement show. "What do you think, Michael?"

With a subtle smile in her direction, Michael turned back to the boys. He studied each of them, long and hard. "Are you willing to take an oath never to repeat what I tell you today?" he asked finally.

Jolene stifled a grin. The boys' heads bobbed up and down like chickens pecking at grain.

"Repeat after me," said Michael, raising one hand as they'd done when they'd taken their school patrol oaths. The three boys did the same, standing tall and rigid. "I solemnly promise," began Michael.

"I solemnly promise," echoed the voices of Reg, Edward and Flynn.

"Never to disclose to anyone—"

"Never to disclose to anyone—"

"In any form — verbal, written or other — anything divulged to me today."

The boys repeated Michael's words, their faces solemn and serious. They ended with a passionate, "So help me God."

Jolene coughed. She was having trouble keeping a straight face, but it was obvious that Michael had everything under control. "All right," he said gesturing for them to form a tight circle around him. Jolene and Cassie hung back on the outer edge. "Just yesterday, I learned that the Germans are planning a massive offensive in the spring — before the troops from the United States swarm into Europe. But we'll be ready for them. We'll stave off that assault and then it will be our turn, with our Canadian troops acting as the lead assault troops. It will take some time to organize, so the plan is not to strike until the summer months. But when we do, it will be a series of victories beginning at the Marne River and ending in the Belgium city of Mons."

"That's the same city that the Germans attacked and took in 1914!" exclaimed Reg.

Jolene was impressed with their knowledge of the Great War, especially her brother's.

"We'll take it back," said Michael. "And by November, the Germans will have surrendered."

"I knew it," shouted Flynn. "Victory will be ours."

"Shh!" warned Jolene, glancing over her shoulder. She took a deep breath and whispered, "You've been entrusted with top-secret information. If this knowledge were to fall into enemy hands . . ." She paused dramatically.

"Have no fear," breathed Edward. "Nothing could make us break our oath."

Jolene pressed her lips together, hemming in her laughter. "Good!" She turned back towards her brother. "Michael, we're due to rendezvous with Gramps at three o'clock sharp."

"Right." He turned to face the boys. "A promise is a debt," he quoted.

The boys raced towards their bicycles and took off. Cassie stood transfixed, a look of raw admiration on her face. "You're so, so brave," she whispered. "Both of you." She placed one hand over her heart. "I have to go to the store for Beth, but promise me you'll come tomorrow after school."

"We'll be here," said Michael, reaching for her free hand and holding her long delicate fingers in his. "If we're able."

Cassie's eyes locked with Jolene's. "I'll see you soon, Jolene." She clutched the folds of her skirt, then turned and ran.

"'If we're able?'" quipped Jolene, rolling her eyes. "I hope you're planning to take drama next year."

Michael laughed. "Did you see their faces, Jo? They bought it all." He paused. "Good idea, sis."

"We were pretty convincing," admitted Jolene.

"Pretty convincing?" protested Michael. "We were awesome. We totally sucked them in."

"Cassie too," she reminded him.

"I know." Michael grinned sheepishly. "I wonder what Mom will think when she finds out she's supposed to be a top-secret war scientist."

"Never mind," mumbled Jolene. "She's not going to. And next time, take off your watch."

Michael chuckled and checked the time. "Come on," he called. "Let's go find Gramps."

Chapter Thirteen

≈

They caught sight of Grandpa almost as soon as they entered the North Street Railway Station. He was leaning against a pillar, chatting to a tall, thin soldier. Sunbeams streamed through the glass roof streaking the faces of the people assembled in the station. Some rested on benches, others clutched suitcases and coats or lingered in line-ups. The long whistle of a train pierced the air and Jolene heard an engine roar to life. She darted to Grandpa's side with Michael close behind.

"Can't say I know the street exactly, but the Richmond area is just north along Campbell Road," Grandpa said, addressing the young soldier. He smiled at the twins. "Perhaps my grandchildren can tell you more." His hand gestured towards the soldier who was dressed in a khaki green jacket and matching britches. "Private Forrester is looking for Roome Street in Richmond. You wouldn't happen to know where that might be, would you?"

"Oh yes," said Jolene, recognizing the street as Cassie's. "It's just a block off Campbell Road near Mulgrave Park. We can take you there if you like." She looked expectantly at Grandpa.

"Sure," he said smoothing his moustache. "We're going in that direction anyway."

The soldier removed his khaki cap, which had a red pin-feather centered over the hat badge, and bowed slightly towards her. "Why thank you. I'm afraid that I'm a bit slow on account of this bad leg of mine, but if you're not in a hurry, I'd be much obliged." He raised the cane that he held in his hand and for the first time, Jolene noticed the artificial leg beneath the cloth wraps that reached from his black lace-up boots to his knee. Balancing with his cane, he took a stiff, awkward step forward.

They passed out of the magnificent doors of the railway station and started down Campbell Road. "Do you have relatives here?" asked Grandpa.

Private Forrester stopped. He leaned on his cane and rested. "No sir. I'm looking for the Caldwell place."

Michael looked up quickly. "Caldwell?" That was Cassie's last name.

"Yes," said Private Forrester. "I'm looking for the family of James Caldwell."

Jolene stared at her boots. "Uh, James Caldwell is dead," she said solemnly.

The soldier nodded. "I know, miss. I was there when it happened." A lump formed in Jolene's throat. She forced herself to look up. "You see," said the young man reaching into his pocket and extracting a small brown envelope, "I've come to return some of his personal belongings to his parents."

Jolene looked away. The contents of that small, brown envelope were all that was left of Cassie's brother. It was a terrible thought and yet, she knew, they were irreplaceable and would be treasured for years to come. Jolene had a sudden recollection of the elderly woman they had helped in the Calgary airport.

She turned at the sound of Michael's voice beside her. "You were with him at Passchendaele." It was a statement not a question, but the soldier saw fit to answer.

"I was," he said.

"I've heard it was a nightmare," said Grandpa.

"One that haunts me nightly," Private Forrester replied. He swung his artificial leg forward over the cobblestones.

"What was it like?" asked Michael.

"There was mud, sludge and slimy pools everywhere. We couldn't roll the big guns through it. Even the horses couldn't manage." The private sighed. "Our battalion was working transportation and we were under continuous shelling, bullets whizzing by, gas shells exploding." Dread

took hold of Jolene. "It was pouring rain and we were laying planks for artillery. James hadn't been sleeping well. We
were all exhausted." He paused and smiled sadly. "I remember looking up one minute and he was there working beside me. The next time I looked back, his body was lying
face down in the muddy water of a shell-hole."

"He'd been shot?" Michael voiced the question on Jolene's
lips.

The private shook his head. "No, he'd fallen exhausted
into the shell-hole and drowned."

"He couldn't swim?" asked Michael.

Private Forrester shrugged. "More likely he couldn't pull
himself up the slippery mud incline. None of us heard
him cry for help." He sighed. "We had a saying that sort of
summed things up. 'He died in Hell. They called it Passchendaele.'"

Nobody spoke. Jolene pressed her fingertips together, her
mind spinning. Where was the glory and honour in drown-
ing in a shell-hole? What would Cassie and her family do
when they heard the tragic story of James' death?

Grandpa put a hand on her shoulder. "Every man did his
part," he said simply. They walked in silence to the corner
of Roome Street.

Michael stopped. His shoulder bumped against Jolene's.
"When Cassie's mom hears how James died..." he began in
a whisper.

"Don't!" said Jolene, struggling with those same thoughts.

"Don't even think about it." She whirled around to face the private. "This is their street," she announced. She marched up the hill and stopped in front of the familiar white wooden structure where Missy's dog was lying on the doorstep. "And this is their house."

Private Forrester joined her. "Thank you," he said kindly. He shook hands with Grandpa just as Cat leaped towards Jolene from behind a tree.

"Cat," she said, hugging the cat's soft body to hers and taking comfort in the creature's warmth. "I'm going to take her around back and see if I can get a glimpse of the kittens," she said, grateful for a chance to escape. She disappeared, leaving Grandpa and Michael to say goodbye to Private Forrester.

Cassie jumped as Jolene came around the corner of the house. "Jolene!" A half-folded apron dangled from her hands. "You scared me. I thought you'd gone to meet your grandfather."

Jolene let Cat jump from her arms. She hesitated, wondering whether or not she should tell Cassie about Private Forrester. It would certainly soften the shock of seeing the young soldier. But it wouldn't diminish the heartbreak or despair. And yet, Private Forrester had brought James' things. Those might offer the family some small consolation. She caught a quick breath then blurted out her news. "I, uh, we met a soldier who served with your brother," she stammered. "He was trying to find his way to your house."

Cassie's blue eyes widened. "He has some things that belonged to James." Jolene's voice died.

Cassie clutched the apron to her face. "I don't want to hear about it." Tears glistened in her eyes.

"I'm, I'm sorry," said Jolene quickly. "I know how hard it must be."

Cassie took a step backwards. "You think you do," she said, "but you have no idea." Tears trickled down her cheeks. "Try to imagine," she said staring into Jolene's eyes, "what it would be like if Michael was killed." She turned and dashed into the house, the back door thudding shut behind her.

Jolene stared at the closed door. What would it be like to wake up one morning and discover that Michael was no longer there? To no longer have a twin? And yet, that was what she had longed for since they'd come on this trip. More space. More time without him. A chance to discover her real self in a world without Michael. Her insides burned with guilt as she made her way back to the front yard.

"I guess we better go," said Grandpa as she joined them. "Life goes on."

Jolene wondered if Cassie's family would be able to go on. They had already endured so much loss and tragedy. She shivered as the breeze gusted. Tonight, they would have to endure more and soon . . . She glanced out towards the harbour. Soon, tragedy would strike even closer to home. And there was nothing she could do about it. She closed her eyes, wishing she had never passed through the time crease into 1917.

"Can I try to take us through the crease?" asked Michael as they approached the hot shadows beside the church on Kaye Street. Grandpa nodded. "One location in time," whispered Michael. Jolene felt her body stretched, then released. "Time is passing over me," said Michael trying to envision the time crease. A hot breeze hit Jolene and her skin grew taut and tight. She reached out a hand and grabbed her brother's arm.

Chapter Fourteen

"Now I know why they say that you can't come all the way to Nova Scotia and not see Peggy's Cove!" exclaimed Dad. They were driving home after having spent the day exploring the granite cliffs and lighthouse at Peggy's Cove.

Michael sat next to Jolene, his face unusually sullen. For the hundredth time that day, he glanced at his watch. "How much farther?" he asked testily.

"I've arranged to pick Mom up at the university and we've got reservations at a great seafood restaurant near the wharf. You can have shrimp or lobster or crab or whatever you fancy." Dad was in good spirits. "After that, I thought we'd spend some time at the Maritime Museum of the Atlantic before heading home."

Jolene watched her brother's face. "Can't you just take me home?" he pleaded. But Dad refused to be persuaded. Jolene said nothing. Michael, she knew, was anxious to return to Richmond. He had promised Cassie that they would, but it would be too late when they reached home.

By the time they had eaten and reached the museum, Michael was tense and irritable. Jolene ambled upstairs, checking out a display on the Titanic and trying to interest him in shipwreck artifacts.

"Come here, you two," called Grandpa as they returned to the main level. "There's an exhibit about the explosion." Jolene and Michael hustled towards a central area that housed the Halifax explosion exhibit. Panoramic views of Richmond before and after the explosion lined the walls. Artifacts found among the ruins lay behind the glass: scribblers, scarves, boots, schoolbags, hatpins, pencil stubs, combs, erasers. Remnants of the ship were on display. "The film's starting," said Grandpa, motioning for them to join him in a small theatre.

Photos flashed on the screen. The morning of Thursday, December 6, 1917. The *Imo,* carrying blankets and relief items for the victims of the war. The *Mont Blanc* with 2400 tons of explosives in her hold, moving into the harbour to await convoy across the Atlantic. Whistles, horns, shouts. The collision. Metal on metal — sparks. Barrels of benzol bursting into smoky flames. Hordes of people gathering to watch. Ships rushing to aid the vessel.

The screen went dark. The sound of an explosion ripped through the theatre.

More photos flashed. Railway tracks twisted and bent. The shattered remains of the sugar refinery. The North Street Railway Station in ruins. The Richmond School crumbling. Houses without windows, doors, roofs.

Residents of Richmond told stories of being swept away by wind, pinned by beams, trapped in houses ignited by their coal-burning stoves. Hot, flying metal shards pierced their skin, severed their limbs. Panes of window glass exploded, scarring them for life.

More scenes on the screen. Soldiers carrying people on stretchers. Wagons loaded with the injured. Relatives searching the hospitals for family members. Mass funerals for the dead.

The audience, including Jolene and Michael, remained sitting as the credits rolled. Finally, they stood up and shuffled out the exit behind Grandpa. Michael paused in front of a map of Richmond. "I didn't realize that so much of the city was affected. I thought that since the ship was in the harbour, the explosion would just have destroyed the other ships and maybe the dock area."

"Those were the people hardest hit," acknowledged Grandpa.

A museum guide had come up behind them. "Those closest to Pier 6 who weren't shielded from the blast were incinerated by the initial fireball," he informed them. "Many of them just disappeared."

Michael turned towards the young man. "How much of Richmond was destroyed?"

"That varied depending on how far away things were from the ship." The guide drew a small circle around the *Mont Blanc* with his finger. "In this area, the explosion produced battering force winds with a powerful vacuum at their centre. The speed of those winds was greater than the speed of sound. People there who weren't protected from the blast were killed by the force before they even heard the explosion."

He indicated the Richmond Railyards that Jolene had visited. "Locomotives and freight cars were hurled like toys. Railroad tracks were ripped up and twisted like pretzels. The winds were seven times greater than the severest hurricanes the world has known."

Jolene closed her eyes. Cassie's father worked in the railyards.

The guide continued. "Those structures that survived the first impact were hit by the vacuum that followed. The air inside those buildings exploded outwards into the vacuum." He pointed at a nearby picture showing a house whose walls protruded outwards. "As well, the *Mont Blanc* burst into tiny shards of shrapnel that rained down on the area. And, as if they needed anything else, the explosion caused a tidal wave that hit the shore and carried many bodies away. For those people close by, the odds of surviving were poor."

"And for those farther away?" asked Michael, his eyes fixed on Roome Street. Jolene looked desperately at Grandpa, who was solemnly combing his moustache.

"A little farther from the blast, especially up on the hill where the houses were unprotected, almost all of the buildings were totally demolished and many people were trapped inside. Some of them managed to dig their way out, but unfortunately their stoves often ignited the wooden wreckage and they died in the fires."

Jolene turned her back to the guide. Cassie's house was part way up that hill. She took a deep breath and exhaled, trying to calm her fears.

"Richmond is built on a steep hill. Some of the wind deflected upwards while some rolled under itself causing a tornado effect. People and bits of the wreckage were picked up and swirled about before being deposited back on the ground."

Jolene stood silently, picturing a tornado in an already devastated area.

"Of course," he continued, "the force of the wind lessened over distance. In the areas of Richmond farthest from the explosion, the houses sustained less damage. Roofs were ripped off and windows shattered, but most houses remained standing. Unfortunately, many of the people who had been standing at those windows watching the burning ship were scarred by the exploding glass." His pager beeped and he pulled it from his pocket. "Within minutes of the explosion, Richmond lay in ruins," he concluded before stepping away to answer the page.

Michael's eyes widened. "Roome Street?" he asked purposefully.

Grandpa pursed his lips and Jolene turned back to the map. "Devastated," came Grandpa's honest answer.

Michael whirled around to face Jolene. "We have to go back." His whisper thundered through the museum. "Cassie and her family could die." Jolene diverted her eyes from his.

"Michael, you can't change history." Grandpa's voice was slow and measured. "As much as we'd like to make a difference and save lives — we can't." Fatigue showed on his face. "Believe me, I've tried, but the simple fact is that even though you can travel back in time, you can't change what happened back then."

"You mean you're just going to stay here and let them die?" Michael's voice was strong and accusing.

"We can't do anything else," said Jolene faintly. "But not everyone died."

"You're unbelievable!" Anger coloured Michael's voice. "I'm going back. I don't care what you do."

"No!" Jolene had rarely heard Grandpa so adamant. "You are not going back, Michael. It's too dangerous." He placed one hand on Michael's wrist. "Yesterday when we were there, it was Tuesday, December 4th. The explosion occurred on the morning of the 6th. You are not going back." Michael opened his mouth to protest, but Grandpa cut him off. "Our time crease is right in the middle of the area that was destroyed by the explosion. You saw the film. Who knows what could happen to you if you went back." Grandpa narrowed his eyes. "I forbid you! Do you understand?"

Michael looked towards Jolene. "It's true, Michael. Gramps and I were almost buried by the rockslide in Frank."

"Frank who?" asked Dad, peering over Jolene's shoulder, but not waiting for a response. "Mom and I have seen all we want to see. Anyone for a drink?"

Sipping her pop, Jolene watched her brother. He was standing at the edge of the wharf, gazing out at the lights of the ferry on the water. She put one hand on his shoulder. "It's the hardest thing about being able to time travel," she said empathetically. "But there's nothing we can do. I guess history has to unfold as history unfolded."

Michael made no response. Jolene let her hand fall.

Chapter Fifteen

T he door clicked. Through groggy eyes, Jolene saw Michael step inside and close the door against the morning sun. He dropped a pile of clothes on the floor and began sorting through them. She propped herself up on one elbow and yawned. "What are you doing? What time is it?"

Michael pulled his woolen trousers over his shorts and his shirt over his swim-club t-shirt. "I'm going back. I hope it's not too late."

Jolene sat bolt upright. "Michael, you can't! You promised Gramps."

"Watch me!" He plunged his arms through the sleeves of his jacket and stepped into his hiking boots. There was an urgency in his movements that unnerved Jolene.

She leaped to her feet and pulled her skirt and blouse

from the pile of clothing. Grandpa was nowhere to be seen. He was probably out for his morning walk. She pulled the garments on over her pyjama shorts and top. Dad had already left to take Mom to her conference. "You heard Gramps," she pleaded. "You could be walking into a disaster."

"A disaster that could kill Cassie, Reg, Beth and her unborn baby." Michael grabbed his cap and flung the door open.

Jolene jammed her bare feet into her boots, not bothering to find her coat or hat. "Wait. Wait for me," she cried, running her fingers through her unbrushed hair and racing after him.

Michael sprinted up the street towards the church and reached the time crease before her. Jolene watched him step into the dense shadows before being totally absorbed. She rushed after him into the hot, dense air. She felt her body stretch in the darkness and a tremendous pressure steal her breath. Then suddenly she was thrown free of the time crease into a sunny December morning in 1917.

Michael had pulled his cap squarely on and was scanning the harbour below them when she joined him, breathless. Numerous ships traversed the water and together they searched the water.

"There!" Michael raised his arm and pointed towards the Narrows just beyond Pier 6. Jolene's eyes followed his outstretched hand and the two of them stood like statues erected on the hillside. From their vantage point, they could see the *Mont Blanc*. Just metres away from her was the *Imo*, steaming forward on a path of collision. Whistles shrieked, horns blew. In desperation, the *Mont Blanc* veered. The prow of the *Imo* ploughed into the munitions ship's deck.

Jolene stared at the two vessels locked in an odd sort of embrace. Slowly, they pulled apart, metal screeching against metal and emitting a shower of sparks. "The benzol is in barrels on the deck," whispered Jolene. As if on cue, the flammable liquid ignited, throwing a dark billowing cloud of smoke into the air. A barrel exploded, shooting ribbons of fire into the clouds of steam and smoke. A kaleidoscope of colours swirled in the sky. Another barrel exploded into spectacular fireworks, then another and another.

"Come on!" cried Michael, racing down the hill.

Jolene watched him in horror. "No!" she screamed. "Michael, stop!"

But her words were lost in the deafening roar of the fire and the shouts of the people now pouring onto the streets. A column of oily black smoke towered above the ship. Balls of fire ripped through it, dispersing into showers of light. Jolene dashed after her brother. By the time she'd reached Campbell Road, she could feel her skin tighten in the incredible heat of the burning ship. Fire bells clanged and a fire engine raced past her. She caught sight of Michael trying to manoeuvre through the crowd and sprinted after him. Hundreds of people were flocking to the dock. Some of the serious spectators had climbed to the top of the fifteen-storey sugar refinery for a bird's eye view of the burning *Mont Blanc,* which was now drifting towards Pier

6. Jolene finally caught up with her brother as the crowd blocked his way. Cries and exclamations went up from the throng as if they were at a carnival. Michael climbed onto a large wooden crate and Jolene scrambled up behind him. From there, they could clearly see the burning ship.

Jolene grabbed Michael's jacket. Heat seared her face and fear clung to her. "Michael, we have to get out of here. Now!"

Michael whirled around to face her, his eyes bright and alive. "You're right," he shouted over the explosive crackling of the flames. Relief flooded over Jolene. She let go of his jacket. "We'll never get to Roome Street this way. We have to find another route." Jolene watched in disbelief as he leaped from the crate, dodged two sailors and bolted back across the cobblestones of Campbell Road up the hill. She tore after him, sidestepping around the motorcars that had ground to a halt in the street. A horse reared, terror in its eyes.

Jolene followed Michael as he turned right on Albert Street and raced onwards. At the corner of Mulgrave Park, he paused to watch the burning ship in the harbour. Another vessel had come alongside, probably intending to tow her away from the pier. A boy on a bicycle screeched to a stop in front of Michael as Jolene caught up with him. "Hey Michael," called Reg. "I bet you've never seen the likes of this." His voice resounded with excitement. "That ship has a cannon on board. I'll wager it's carrying ammunition." He stood up and pedalled furiously down the hill.

"Reg!" called Michael, but the boy was gone, his cap flying off his head.

Jolene gripped Michael's arm. She was panting and sweat soaked her blouse. "Please," she pleaded. "We have to go back. That ship's going to explode." Desperation ran deep in her words.

For a moment, her brother hesitated. "I don't want Cassie to die," he shouted. He wrenched himself free of her grip and started to race across Mulgrave Park.

"Yeah, well I don't want you to die," she screamed after him.

At that instant, Jolene was acutely aware of an ominous unnatural silence. A blinding flash illuminated the world and simultaneously she heard the ear-splitting boom of an explosion. A blast of air swept her forward and sent her crashing to the earth. Looking up, she caught sight of an enormous mushroom cloud. Something struck her head and pain racked her body. Her head slumped and her eyes closed. "Michael," she whispered as the world turned black.

Blackness gave way to swirls of light. Jolene tried to open her eyes. Her eyelashes were stuck together with greasy black soot. She blinked the grimy substance away, aware of a sharp pain above her ear. Her head was sore and tender to touch. Jolene tried to sit up but pain pulsed in her right leg. Ignoring it, she managed to push herself into a sitting position. Shingles and tree branches covered her legs. Grimy oil seeped into her mouth and she spat. Lifting her left hand from a pile of shattered glass, she brushed the debris off her stomach and chest. From somewhere nearby came a woman's muffled screams.

"Michael," she called tentatively, looking over the area. Piles of rubble dotted the landscape. Fragments of homes, trees and furniture littered the ground around her. Jolene reached out and picked up a broken picture frame. Half of a child's face smiled back at her. She let it drop and swept the branches and shingles off her legs. Blood trickled from a cut below her knee. Ignoring it, she staggered to her feet, glass from the folds of her skirt tinkling to the earth.

"Michael." Unsteadily she turned in a circle, taking in her surroundings. She was standing in what appeared to have once been a backyard. To her right, a pile of kindling was all that was left of a house. The roof was in shambles across the street. Jolene picked her way through the wreckage — slabs of wood, scattered chimney bricks, a twisted bicycle. Across the way, a man was tearing at the broken beams of a home that resembled a beaver dam. A moan escaped from the pile of sticks. Someone was trapped inside.

Jolene stumbled into the street, her head pounding. She had to find her brother. The last thing she remembered was watching him race across Mulgrave Park. An open field lay just below her on the hill and she hurried in that direction. The field was strewn with branches and boards. She swerved to avoid the tiny body of a dead bird and felt panic overcome her. "Michael!" she cried loudly. "Michael! Michael!"

Running frantically through the rubble, she searched through the debris, all the time calling his name. Where was he? Why didn't he answer her? A grove of trees in the far corner of the park had been levelled and she fled towards it, her voice desperate and searching. "Michael! Michael!" Was he hurt or even worse . . . "Michael!"

"Jo." A hand waved feebly from amidst the broken tree trunks.

Lifting her skirt, Jolene leaped over the branches, twigs slapping at her legs and tripping her up. He was pinned to the ground by an uprooted tree but he was alive. "Michael," she breathed in relief. She knelt on the ground beside him. His green eyes peered up at her and a white smile gleamed momentarily in his black, tarred face. "Are you hurt?"

Michael strained to see his left shoulder, which was pinned to the ground. "I'm not sure." He struggled to move. "I'm, I'm trapped."

Jolene scrambled to her feet, pulling branches and debris away from her brother. "How did you get here?" she asked him. "When I last saw you, you were in the middle of the park."

Michael grimaced as Jolene continued to clear away the twigs and objects covering him. "The wind picked me up and hurled me head over heels through the air. Branches and bits of metals flew past me. When I hit the ground, I was here in the middle of these trees."

"That must have been the tornado effect we heard about." Jolene shoved a large branch to the ground and inspected the trunk that held her brother captive. "That's a big tree." Gripping it with both hands, she attempted to shove it off him, but it would not move. Michael tried to pull away from underneath it, but it was impossible. Jolene tried again, this time using her legs to exert pressure on the large trunk. Michael used his free hand against it as well, but it was too heavy. "I can't budge it," Jolene said.

Michael's eyes closed.

"Hang on." Jolene scampered across the street and returned moments later dragging a long, heavy piece of wood that looked like it had once been part of a doorframe. Jamming it under the tree trunk, she positioned herself at the other end of the lever. Michael nodded encouragingly as she pushed down on it, straining with every muscle in her body. The trunk shifted and Michael squirmed. Jolene, her face red with exertion, applied more force and the tree lifted. Michael scuttled sideways, pulling his arm free as the tree thudded back to the ground.

Jolene stood panting beside her brother. His arms were as black as his face and for the first time, she realized that he was not wearing his cap, shirt or jacket. Only his swim club t-shirt remained. His trousers had also been shredded.

Michael scrambled to his feet, clutching his shoulder. He reached up and plucked a twig from her hair. "Are you okay?" he asked, his voice cracking.

Jolene pointed at his shoulder. "Is it broken?"

Cautiously, Michael lifted his arm, rotating it in a large

circle. "It's sore, probably bruised, but I don't think it's broken." His eyes misted over and his lower lip trembled. Without warning, his long arms encircled Jolene in a crushing embrace. "Jo, I'm so sorry. I've been so stupid. You could have been killed."

Jolene pressed her head against his chest. "And after the way I've acted lately, I don't suppose you'd mind," she said apologetically. She looked up at him, their eyes meeting in a look that needed no words. Finally, Jolene cleared her throat. "Anyway, we're both fine."

They surveyed the scene. "It's lucky we were as far away from the ship as we were," she said.

"And in the park away from most buildings," added Michael.

In every direction, the city lay in ruins, shattered by the force of the explosion. Michael heard the sound of water and turned to look. A wave of ocean water was cresting towards them, beginning its climb up Richmond Hill. They jumped up onto a pile of wood and furniture as the tidal wave seeped across the frozen ground, losing force on the hill above them and gradually passing back down towards the harbour.

A mother clutching a silent infant hurried past them. Another woman, her face bleeding, one foot dragging behind her stumbled into the street beside them. "The Germans have attacked. The Germans have attacked," she muttered over and over again. Jolene didn't bother to correct her.

The smell of smoke diverted her attention. Lazy tendrils curled upwards from a heap of sticks across the street that had once been a home. The wood crackled and tongues of flame licked the rubble. A piercing scream rose from within.

"The stoves," Jolene murmured. The flames leaped higher.

A motorcar rolled to a stop beside them and soldiers spilled out of its doors. "Get out of here," ordered one of them. "Can't you see the flames?"

Michael caught Jolene's hand and pulled her away from the burning house. Terrified, they stumbled back into the park. Only the thinnest saplings remained standing, lonely sentinels guarding the devastation. Below Mulgrave Park, the frame of a house still stood, its beams protruding as if it had exploded from the inside out. Its roof, windows and doors were missing. Jolene spun about searching for the street that bordered the park — Roome Street.

"It's over there," said Michael, pointing. "But there's nothing left. I guess it was too high on the hill."

Cassie's house, like the ones they had seen higher on the hill, had been reduced to a pile of sticks. Despondency rose within Jolene as they made their way towards the ruins. A tiny figure hobbled towards them and Jolene recognized Mrs. Noseworthy. "They're in there!" she shrieked.

Jolene's heart surged. Two soldiers and a blackened young man tugged feverishly at the wreckage, sending boards clattering to the ground. Jolene lunged forward, but Michael restrained her. Flames flickered and smoke drifted upwards. A dog barked from inside the collapsed house.

"The baby, too," stammered Mrs. Noseworthy. "She was standing in the doorway holding him, seeing the others off to school."

"What?" demanded Michael, watching the men work frantically on the remains of the house.

"The children had just left for school," cried Mrs. Noseworthy. The wind gusted and fed the flames. "Cassie, that dear little Missy and the boy, you know."

Perhaps they were still alive. Fire crackled and engulfed one corner of the wreckage. They had met Reg on his way to the harbour. Perhaps Cassie and Missy had made it safely to school. Jolene stepped back from the flames. If they had, they had almost certainly lost their mother and little Ben. She turned her back on the fiery heat, feeling sick to her stomach.

"Come on," said Michael. "We can't do anything here." He strode up the hill in the direction of Richmond School. Jolene remained, looking back on the burning scene. The soldiers had abandoned their work and stood watching helplessly as the flames consumed the house.

Jolene's knees buckled. She sank to the ground. "Meow." The plaintive cry made her jerk her head upwards. Out of the corner of her eye, she caught sight of a movement. The shed in the backyard had been blown apart. Two tiny kittens huddled together on the edge of the rubble.

Slowly, she crept towards the tiny balls of fur — one ginger with two white ears and the other a deeper orange with three white socks. "Where's Cat?" she whispered. The kittens shrank back as the heat from the fire became more intense. Cat was nowhere to be seen. Jolene scooped the trembling kittens up. They meowed loudly then purred.

Michael reappeared seconds later. "What are you doing? The fire's spreading!"

Jolene held the kittens out to him. "We can't leave them. They'll die."

For a moment, Michael looked at her as if she were truly crazy. "All right," he said, taking the ginger-coloured one from her. "Let's go."

Clutching the kitten, Jolene fled after Michael. "Richmond School should be right there," she said as they climbed the hill. Injured people stumbled through the streets all around them and smoke engulfed the daylight.

Michael raised one hand and pointed. "Is that it?"

The large two-storey stone structure lay in ruins. Only a portion of the outside wall was still standing. A young woman with a school-aged child wandered past them. "Were all the students killed?" Jolene asked, numb with horror.

The woman, glass embedded in her cheeks, shook her head. "I wouldn't suppose there were many of them there yet," she replied. "The new winter hours started this week. They didn't go in until 9:30." Michael glanced at his watch. It had stopped at 9:04.35.

The woman limped ahead as a horse-drawn wagon clattered past them. "You kids hurt?" asked a man in uniform, jumping down to talk to them. Injured people lay on the back of the wagon.

A cold wind gusted and Jolene shivered. "No, we're okay," she said. "There are others who need your help more."

The soldier removed the long, heavy coat he wore and draped it around Jolene's shoulders. "I wish I had another," he told Michael, before leaping back into the wagon.

Jolene was grateful for the warmth of the coat. "We can share," she told her brother.

"I'm fine," said Michael, "but this little guy might like a warm spot." He slipped the shivering kitten into the deep pocket of the coat and Jolene did the same with the one she carried. Contented purrs emanated from the creatures as they snuggled together.

"I guess we ought to go back." Michael gestured helplessly. "We'll never find them now."

Were Cassie and Missy still alive? And what about Reg and Beth and Rory? Jolene tried not to think about what might have happened to them. She closed her eyes, buried her fingers in the soft fur of the kittens and followed Michael.

Chaos and destruction were everywhere on Albert Street. A dog lay dead at the base of a picket fence. People with bloody gashes and broken limbs stood sobbing as their homes burned. Michael turned towards the harbour, moving against the stream of people climbing the hill. Some carried possessions — a clock, an iron, a scribbler decorated with drawings of war ships.

Campbell Road was oddly empty. The cables for the tram lay like snakes across the cobblestones. Close to the exploding ship, the wharf had been swept clear of debris. They passed the railyards. The iron pedestrian bridge had been torn free and lay twisted not far away. Boxcars had been flipped upside down and locomotives lay on their side, like the abandoned contents of a child's toybox.

The wharves where the stevedores had loaded and unloaded goods were bare and empty, but a massive pile of wreckage marked the location of the Acadia Sugar Refinery. Two men, carrying a stretcher, were struggling near a half-anchored lamppost.

"Unhand me. Do ye not hear?" Rory's unmistakable voice boomed from the midst of the group.

"We have to get you to a hospital." Rory's great frame whirled around and flung one man to the ground. He staggered away from them, his hair plastered to his head, his clothes, dripping wet.

"Rory?" asked Jolene peering at him.

He tripped towards her, seemingly unaware of the blood that gushed from a wound on his thigh. One arm hung limply at his side and a portion of his beard was missing. "You've seen my Beth, lass?" he asked, recognizing her immediately.

Jolene shook her head. "No," she stammered, "but I think she was going to volunteer at the hospital this morning."

Rory stopped walking. "Well, I'll be, lass. I'll be. Ye're right. She told me the same but I'd forgot. My Beth's at the hospital."

"That's where you ought to be," said Michael, staring at Rory's bloodstained pants.

A smile crossed the great man's face. "So it is." He turned to the men who had been trying to convince him to get on the stretcher. "So what are ye waiting for?" he roared, sitting down on the canvas. "Take me to the hospital." He laid his head back and within seconds was unconscious.

The stretcher-bearers strained under his weight. "Think he'll make it?" asked one.

The other man laughed. "He'll make it all right. I heard he stayed to help batten down the hatches of the *S.S. Picton.* There's explosives aboard and they were afraid the ship would catch on fire. They finished just seconds before the explosion and ran for cover." He adjusted the handles of the stretcher. "He shouldn't have lived through this, but he did."

"Must have been shielded from the explosion by the refinery."

The two men started to move towards a motorcar. "The part I can't believe is how, with all these injuries, he clung to that lamppost when the tidal wave hit the wharf. I think he just refused to die."

Jolene stood silently beside Michael. Maybe Rory had refused to die or maybe he'd just been lucky. Jolene wasn't sure but she was confident that Rory would survive. He would find Beth at the hospital and take her and their baby to his beloved Cape Breton in the spring.

Despite the layers of smoke, Jolene could feel snow in the air. Michael shuddered as an icy wind gusted off the harbour. "I sure hope Beth's all right," he said gently. "She's the only reason he goes on living."

Jolene nodded in agreement. "We'd better go." They dragged themselves past smashed buildings and sprawled corpses, trying not to look. Rescue crews patrolled the streets, but here, close to Pier 6, the devastation and death were virtually complete. As they passed the Protestant Orphanage, Jolene noticed that the building had been completely shattered. She glanced down at her torn skirt and blouse. Nobody there would be needing them now.

Trudging up Kaye Street, Jolene felt fatigue overcome her. Her knee throbbed and her head and blistered feet ached. None of the homes on the street was distinguishable. She heard Michael stop beside her and looked up at a pile of ruins. The church had been decimated. A heap of rubble lay where the time crease had been. Terror struck Jolene. She searched the perimeter of the wreckage for the hot, tangible air that marked energy trapped in time. Nothing! The time crease had been buried. Slowly she raised her eyes to Michael. His eyes mirrored her fear.

Chapter Sixteen

"Hey, you there!" A man on horseback galloped towards them. "Get out of here. Hurry. The ammunition in the magazine's going to blow." He gestured wildly in the direction of Wellington Barracks. "Quickly, get to high ground."

The urgency of his voice set their feet in motion. Jolene and Michael ran up the hill, away from the barracks. Others abandoned the wreckage of their homes and darted to high ground, fearing another explosion. They followed the galloping horseman towards high, open ground at the top of a large knoll. Jolene recognized it as Fort Needham, where she and Grandpa had first met the soldier who had been blinded by gas. It seemed like years ago now.

Hundreds of people had assembled there, many injured

and awaiting transportation to hospitals. Jolene and Michael swerved among them. People with eyes covered by strips of petticoats. People with makeshift splints and slings. Those that were able to help had tried to make them comfortable with whatever could be found. Now they moved among the wounded offering blankets, coats and words of assurance.

A girl about her own age, her head bandaged, cradled a small child. Jolene stopped walking. It was Cassie and Missy. Cassie's hair cascaded across the angelic face of her little sister. "Cassie," Jolene called, rushing towards them with Michael close behind.

Cassie's blue eyes glanced upwards. She smiled. "You've come," she said simply. Jolene noticed the awkward angle of her foot and the bloody bandage around her head.

"Yes," said Jolene gently. "Are you hurt?"

Cassie shrugged. With a filthy hand, she caressed the pale skin of her sister whose head lay in her lap. The child appeared to be unharmed, untouched by the cruel hand of disaster. There was not a mark on her body, but her eyes were closed and her chest barely moved. "I'm worried about Missy."

"What happened?" asked Jolene, stroking the child's hair.

"I don't know. I was unconscious and when I came to, she was just lying there — like this." Cassie gripped Jolene's hand. "She can't die, Jolene, she can't." Tears welled up in her blue eyes. "She's such a big part of me."

"Over here!" a starched voice ordered. "You children step away."

Jolene stepped back to make room for a matronly woman who had taken charge of the situation. Cassie's words echoed inside her head. Cassie was her own person but being Missy's sister was a part of her identity just as being Michael's twin was a part of who she was. Why hadn't she been able to see that earlier?

Jolene slid her hand into her coat pocket. The kittens! She'd almost forgotten about them. Missy's kittens.

Two men with a stretcher manoeuvred through the crowd towards Missy. "What happened to her?" asked one of the stretcher-bearers.

Cassie shrugged. "I think she's hurt on the inside." Her voice bordered on tears.

"Probably some internal hemorrhaging," barked the woman as the men set the stretcher down and transferred Missy onto it.

Jolene bent down and picked up Missy's hand. "Missy," she called gently. "Missy, Cat's kittens are here."

The little girl's eyes flickered.

"Look, Missy, the kittens are here."

Missy's eyes slowly opened. She struggled to speak, but could not. Jolene pulled the ginger kitten with the white ears out of her pocket and tucked it against Missy's chest. The kitten meowed in the cold air, but the little girl's delicate fingers encircled it and its complaint changed to a purr. Missy's eyes closed again and she managed a contented smile as the men lifted the stretcher.

Cassie smiled gratefully at Jolene. Tears slid down her

cheeks as Michael helped her to her feet. She steadied herself and reached out one hand to each of them. "Everything's ruined," she said sadly, "all our dreams."

"No," said Jolene. "You're a survivor, like me." She gripped Cassie's arm, knowing she spoke the truth. "Nothing can take that away from us."

Cassie squeezed Jolene's hand as the matronly woman urged her forward. Her eyes flickered to Michael's downcast face and she smiled kindly. "I have to go. I wish we could have spent more time together." Michael could only nod.

Jolene reached inside the pocket of the great coat a second time. "We found two kittens," she said quickly.

"Keep one," replied Cassie. "Missy would like that." They watched Cassie climb aboard the wagon. She raised one hand in farewell as the horse lurched forward.

Jolene studied her brother's distraught face, knowing that his pain and sorrow ran as deep as hers. She could do nothing more for her friend now, but at least Cassie had Missy and Rory and perhaps others. She leaned against her brother, finally understanding her mother's words on the beach. She had Michael. Together they had survived the explosion. Now they just had to find a way to get back home.

"Jo! Michael!" Grandpa swept down on them, wrapping strong arms around them both. "I've been searching everywhere for you!" Jolene buried her head against his shoulder. He released them from his hug, his green eyes glinting with relief, then anger. "You could have been killed. Do you know how foolish it was to come back here?" Before they could answer, he hugged them to him again. "I'm so glad you're safe."

"The time crease is buried," said Michael.

"I know. When I got back from my walk and found you missing, I knew where you'd gone. I tried to go through the time crease by the church, but I couldn't. It was blocked, presumably buried by rubble after the explosion. It was the same all over Richmond. I finally took a cab to the—"

"Citadel," said Jolene, wondering why she hadn't thought to go there earlier.

"Yes," acknowledged Grandpa. "I came through the time crease there."

"Can we get back that way?" asked Michael.

"We can," said Grandpa taking off his jacket and wrapping it around Michael's shoulders. "It's a bit of a walk though."

Hordes of homeless people were moving in the direction of the Citadel, seeking refuge. They joined the long, slow-moving lines.

"Victor!" Grandpa turned as Cassie's father ran towards them. Sweat poured from his face and his eyes were wild and desperate. He stumbled, his chest heaving.

"Are you hurt?" asked Grandpa, supporting the exhausted man.

Cassie's father shook his head. "No. We were just leaving Rockingham on the train when I felt a blast that shook the earth. We pushed on, but the line was blocked. I ran as fast as I could but the soldiers wouldn't let me into the area around our house. There were fires everywhere and they were afraid the magazine at the barracks would explode." He paused to catch his breath, looking from Grandpa to Jolene to Michael. "Have you, by chance, any word of my family?"

Jolene looked down, away from his hopeful eyes. "We saw Cassie and Missy at Fort Needham," she began uncertainly. "A wagon took them to the hospital."

"They're badly hurt?"

Jolene raised her eyes. "Cassie's got a head wound and injured her foot and Missy..." Her voice trailed off. "They're not sure how she is, but she took the kitten I found."

Cassie's father beamed at her. "God bless you," he said. "Any word of Reg or the others?"

Michael cleared his throat. "Last time we saw Reg, he was headed to the dock to watch the burning ship." He hesitated, then continued. "We haven't heard anything official, but I think Beth was at the hospital volunteering and Rory..." He grinned despite the horror around him. "He's hurt, but what could kill Rory?"

Mr. Caldwell nodded. Neither Jolene nor Michael spoke. Cassie's father swallowed and asked the question that Jolene knew he hated to ask. "Have you been by the house? What of Mary and the baby?"

Jolene stroked the kitten in her pocket. How could she find the words to tell this kind, loving man that his wife and child were dead? Grandpa's hand caressed her shoulder. It had taken all his courage to ask. She summoned her nerve. "I'm, I'm afraid that your house was completely destroyed, sir," she said, without looking up. "The neighbours tried to dig through the rubble, but they had to give up because of the flames." She could not go on.

Michael came to her aid. "I'm sorry, Mr. Caldwell. There was nothing anyone could do."

Cassie's father covered his face with his hands. His shoulders heaved and his gentle sobs filled the silence. For what seemed like an eternity, he stood and wept.

Jolene watched the sobbing man. Would he find the courage to go on? To reassemble his family and their shattered dreams? Days ago, she had been unable to understand how anybody could do so in the face of such a disaster. But now, she knew that those with inner strength and courage could. And in the process they just might discover something about themselves, like who or what mattered most to them. Family, she had come to realize, mattered most to her.

Grandpa put a comforting arm around Mr. Caldwell's shoulders. For a while, he said nothing. "I, too, am sorry," he said finally. "I know what it means to lose a wife."

Mr. Caldwell pulled a handkerchief from his pocket and wiped his face. "Perhaps," he said, blowing his nose, "perhaps it's for the best." He looked up with sorrowful eyes. "I don't think she could have withstood any more grief in her life." He gestured around. "Certainly not this."

Jolene recalled the sad, haunted expression of Cassie's mother. At least she had been spared the knowledge that, in all probability, her two remaining sons were dead.

Cassie's father clasped Grandpa's hand and took a deep breath. He drew himself up to his full height. "Well, I'd best be getting over to the hospital." He bade them farewell and Jolene watched him stride away. At least Cassie and Missy had their father and he had them.

"Will they be all right?" asked Michael.

"Tragedy often draws a family closer," replied Grandpa.

Jolene contemplated his remark. Cassie's family had already suffered so many tragedies and they were close and strong. But tragedy could also divide people. She looked affectionately at Michael. "Or maybe it just makes you realize how much you meant to each other even before the tragedy."

"Maybe," echoed Grandpa.

The wind gusted and Jolene pulled the soldier's coat tighter around her shoulders. They walked in silence. As they approached the grassy slopes of the Citadel, Jolene stroked the tiny creature in her pocket. For some reason, it gave her hope.

"Over here," said Grandpa, veering right. People milled about looking for a place to rest, a place to gather and comfort each other. Soldiers carried injured people through the doors of the fort.

"This is what we saw through the window at the Citadel that day," observed Michael, turning in a full circle. Jolene stared at the aftermath of destruction she had already witnessed. Having lived through the explosion gave it a brand new meaning.

Grandpa dug his handkerchief out of his pocket. "Wipe your faces." Jolene and Michael tried to remove the black sludge, but it was too thick and grimy. Grandpa motioned for them to follow him towards a shaded nook in the wall of the Citadel. Jolene felt the air grow warm, thick and electric. Her skin began to tighten and stretch. She strained to clench her fists as the pressure increased, but could not. She struggled to breathe, a heavy weight on her chest. The kitten squirmed and suddenly the darkness gave way to light.

They stood outside the Citadel gasping for air and looking out at the skyscrapers of Halifax. Jolene reached out one hand and touched the rough stone wall. Happiness, like the hot August sun, enveloped her.

Chapter Seventeen

Grandpa flagged down a taxi on the street below the Citadel and Jolene and Michael collapsed onto the back seat. They stared blankly out the windows, leaving Grandpa to respond to the driver's inquiring looks and comments. In front of their rental house on Kaye Street, Grandpa paid the fare and helped them out of the car.

Jolene stood, looking up and down the street. In 1917, the houses on this very street had been blown to bits, but since then, the Richmond area had been rebuilt. With hope and determination, the residents of Richmond had started again.

"Looking at this area now, you'd never know there'd been a disaster," said Grandpa, voicing her thoughts. "After the explosion, soldiers and sailors, many from ships in the harbour, started the rescue work. They spent the entire day pulling people from the rubble and taking the wounded to the hospital."

"Like Missy and Cassie," said Jolene.

Grandpa squinted into the sun. "Of course, there weren't enough beds for everyone, but the medical staff did their best, working long into the night, day after day. Doctors and nurses from all over Nova Scotia came to Halifax to help." He stepped up onto the sidewalk. "Sometimes tragedy brings out the best in people. Help arrived from all over, especially from the United States."

"What about all those people who lost their homes?" asked Michael.

"They stayed in temporary relief shelters — in the Citadel or on the grounds of the Commons. People opened their homes and their hearts."

"Cassie had lots of relatives. Maybe they went to stay with them," said Jolene hopefully.

"Maybe, once their relatives found them." Grandpa continued in response to the twins' puzzled looks. "So many people had died, some without a trace. Others had been taken to wherever they could get help — cities and towns outside of Halifax, Dartmouth by ferry, ships in the harbour, hospitals or shelters throughout the city. Relatives and family members often spent days visiting the hospitals and the morgue, searching for their loved ones. And many of the injured lay in hospitals wondering if any of their kin were still alive."

Jolene's boots scuffed across the sidewalk blocks. "I wonder if Beth was working at the hospital they took Missy and Cassie to."

"At least Mr. Caldwell knew that some of his family had survived," said Michael.

"Thanks to you two. For days and weeks after the explosion, survivors and relatives searched for missing relatives. Some took out ads in the paper and as a result, there were many happy reunions. But other advertisements were never answered." Grandpa paused, before relating the final events of the disaster. "Unfortunately, the weather didn't cooperate either. A storm hit Halifax on the afternoon of the explosion. The next day brought more snow and two days later, a blizzard covered the city in white."

"It was so unfair," said Jolene.

"But the people persevered and eventually they rebuilt their city." Grandpa gestured at their rental house. "The houses, churches and schools were gradually reconstructed, although the Richmond kids had no school until May. They were glad to go back, but many of their friends and schoolmates were missing."

"That would be awful," said Michael. "How would you ever forget about the disaster and go on?"

"I'm not sure if they ever did forget," said Grandpa, placing a strong hand behind each of their shoulders. They climbed the steps to the porch together. "But they did have a chance to say goodbye. For months, funeral services were conducted. Finally the remaining unidentified bodies in the morgue, many of them children, were buried in a mass grave."

"All because two ships collided in the harbour." Michael looked up. "Whose fault was it, Gramps?"

Grandpa leaned against the porch railing. "Nobody was ever charged in connection with the disaster. The *Imo* was supposed to have left the harbour the day before the explosion. But the boat bringing her coal arrived too late in the day and she was forced to lay over. Some say she was travelling too fast when she met the *Mont Blanc*." Grandpa shrugged. "The *Mont Blanc* was originally supposed to travel to Europe from New York. But she was too heavy and was ordered to join a slower convoy in Halifax. She arrived late on the night of the 5th and had to spend the night anchored off McNab's Island. And she should never have been carrying the barrels of benzol on deck. It was far too dangerous." Grandpa rubbed his neck.

"Couldn't they have done anything to prevent the explosion?" asked Jolene.

"Some of the ships in the area tried to battle the blaze and one of the tugs came alongside hoping to tow the burning ship out to sea. Unfortunately, the *Mont Blanc* wasn't flying its red munitions flag, which would have signalled that there were explosives aboard."

"Is that why everyone gathered around to watch instead of running away?" asked Jolene, remembering the carnival-like atmosphere at the pier. "Because they didn't know what was on board the *Mont Blanc*?"

Grandpa nodded. "It was war time. Only a few people knew the fatal secret of the *Mont Blanc*."

"Until she exploded," said Jolene.

"And then it was too late." Michael pressed his fingertips together. "I guess Christmas would have been pretty dismal."

Cassie had been offered the lead in the Christmas play. Jolene smiled at the thought of their first meeting, their shared dreams and laughter. She sat down on the wooden bench and unlaced her boots, gritty with soot. "You know what I can't figure out," she said, pulling a black foot from her boot.

"What?" asked her brother.

"Why fate was so cruel. Cassie had to live through World War One and the Halifax explosion and when she's older, she'll have to endure World War Two."

"But before that, she'll have to survive the Spanish influenza epidemic that killed more Canadians than any other disaster. And then she'll have to face the Great Depression of the 1930s." Grandpa twirled the ends of his moustache.

"Wow!" said Michael. "And all I have to worry about is being a twin . . . sometimes," he added with a guilty glance at his sister.

Jolene stared incredulously at her brother. She flopped back against the arm of the bench in shock. "What! You mean. . ." But her question was interrupted by a loud meow. Jolene's eyes met Michael's. In all the excitement of returning to the present, they had completely forgotten about the tiny creature sleeping in the pocket of her coat.

The kitten meowed again and she pulled it from its hiding place. Its inquisitive green eyes blinked in the sunlight.

Grandpa looked startled. "Well, well," he said, bending over and tapping its white front paws, "what bit of chaos did you two bring home with you?"

"Chaos," repeated Jolene. "That would make a good name for a kitten." She looked hopefully at her brother.

"Chaos," echoed Michael, taking the fuzzy orange kitten from her, "is a very good name." Chaos let out a hungry roar as Jolene returned her brother's smile.

ABOUT THE AUTHOR

Cathy Beveridge was born and raised in Calgary and spent four years abroad in the Middle East. While there, she developed a keen interest in writing Canadian stories and, upon her return to Alberta, wrote *Shadows of Disaster,* the story of Frank Slide, Canada's deadliest landslide. *Shadows of Disaster* was shortlisted for the 2004 Golden Eagle Book Award, Rocky Mountain Book Award and Saskatchewan Young Readers' Choice Diamond Willow Award. While on a recent family vacation to Halifax, the birthplace of her father, Cathy became intrigued by the events and scope of the Halifax explosion. The result was *Chaos in Halifax,* the second adventure in Canadian disasters. Her other publications include a contemporary young adult novel, *Offside* (Thistledown, 2001), winner of the Saskatchewan Young Readers' Choice 2003 Snow Willow Award, as well as numerous stories in young adult anthologies such as *Beginnings: Stories of Canada's Past* (Ronsdale, 2001), *Up All Night* (Thistledown, 2001) and the *Issues Collection* (McGraw-Hill Ryerson, 1994-95). Cathy has also written a Teacher's Guide to accompany *Chaos in Halifax,* which is available from Ronsdale Press.